Essays That Worked

Essays
THAT WORKED

50 Essays from Successful Applications
to the Nation's Top Colleges

Edited by
Boykin Curry and Brian Kasbar

Mustang Publishing
New Haven

Library of Congress Cataloging in Publication Data:
Essays that worked.

    1. College applications--United States. 2. English language--United States--Composition and exercises.
3. Universities and colleges--United States--Admission.
I. Curry, Boykin, 1966-   II. Kasbar, Brian, 1966-   .
LB2351.52.U6E87 1986   808'.042   86-60433
ISBN 0-914457-14-4

10 9 8 7 6 5 4 3 2 1

For God, for Country, and for Yale

and also, of course, for our parents

Acknowledgments

We would like to thank many people.

First and foremost, our sincere thanks to the students who allowed us to publish their essays. They let us expose their most personal thoughts to thousands of readers who may not share their sympathies, backgrounds, or perspectives.

Many admissions officers at many colleges provided us with assistance and encouragement. In particular, thanks to Warren Hodges, Louise Burnham, and Worth David in the Yale Admissions Department, Dan Lundquist at the University of Pennsylvania, John Braunstein at Oberlin, Laura Fisher at Harvard, Steve Lemanager at Princeton, Evelyn Stockton Lane at Williams, Charles Deacon at Georgetown, Rachel Hendrickson at Johns Hopkins, Anne Coxon at Stanford, Kalima Rose at Berkeley, John Hopkins at Grinnel, Catherine Clack at Rice, Mary Jane Crossno at Duke, Tony Strickland at UNC/Chapel Hill, Steve Saud at Davidson, Natalie Aharonian at Wellesley, and Sarah Hecksher at the Springside School.

Thanks to Brenda, Caroline, Marshall, and Wayne—our brothers and sisters—who told all their friends to buy this book.

We could not have finished the book without Fred Strebeigh, a writing professor at Yale, and Tracy Capers, who worked tirelessly on short notice to type our manuscript.

And thanks to our publisher, Rollin Riggs, the only person who would take a chance on two kids who had no idea what they were doing.

Table of Contents

Introduction... 9
An Interview With an Admissions Officer............................. 13
The Essays.. 17
  Essays About the Application Process........................... 19
  Self-Description Essays.. 42
  Realization Essays... 60
  Off-Beat Essays.. 80
  Thought Essays... 92
  Activities Essays...104
  Descriptive Essays..124

Introduction

You are an admissions officer at Harvard, Duke, or Stanford, and it is 2:00 in the morning of April 9. Your desk is somewhere beneath a huge stack of papers. Your eyes are tired and red. Mechanically, you open the next application folder, and again you force yourself to read:

I am constantly striving to expose myself to every opportunity to become a person with a deep understanding of my own values and of the environment in which I find myself. I have participated in a broad range of activities, and I have endeavored to become ever more versatile and tolerant while at the same time solidifying my own ideals . . .

You cannot go on. But you must, because the deadline for notifying applicants is just a few days away. The prospect: another long night reading vague, boring, pompous essays. You slowly bow your head and rest it in your hands, wishing for a different job.

Suddenly, a gust of wind blows through an open window, upsetting the pile of applications. As 400 essays flutter around the room, you notice a page with the recipe for cranberry bread.

A recipe? Cranberry bread?

Curious, you pick up the essay and start to read, and you smile:

4 c. flour
2 c. sugar
3 t. baking powder
1 pkg. cranberries

. . . Not only is the following an overview of my personality but also a delicious recipe.

First the flour and sugar need to be sifted together into a large bowl. Flour reminds me of the powder snow that falls in the West. I was born and raised in Pennsylvania where our snow falls more like sugar, granular and icy, and makes us hardy skiers unlike those spoiled by Western snow. Cold weather is also conducive to reading . . .

Finally, a student you would want to *meet*, someone who dares to express herself creatively, rather than simply recite the same old litany of high school achievements and adolescent philosophies. Finally, an interesting essay!

As you finish the "recipe" and read through the rest of her application, you start to feel much better. Decent grades, good test scores, solid recommendations—you've seen better, but it's certainly respectable. And then there's this fantastic essay, evidence of an inventive and independent mind. The essay makes your decision easy. You put her folder into a box marked "Admit," and you look forward to discussing her with the Admissions Committee tomorrow.

This is an exaggeration, of course, but it makes an important point. Admissions officers are very human. They will laugh at a funny joke, and they will get excited over a well-written account of a close game. They may even shed a tear if you pull them through a tragedy. On the other hand, admissions officers will become bored and irritated as quickly as anyone by essays that are dull and blatantly self-serving.

When we first started working on this book, we collected hundreds of essays. Filled with enthusiasm on our first night, we started reading. Several hours later, after ten class elections, eight trips to Europe, and five solutions to the problem of world hunger, we were praying for an essay that was *fun* to read, an essay that might make us laugh or think or understand. But please, God, not another piece on "what-I-learned-by-working-so-hard-as-yearbook-editor."

We quickly understood why the smallest bit of wit or creativity can strike an admissions officer as exceptional brilliance.

In its own way, each essay in this book is enlightening and entertaining. It informs the reader without boring him. Since these essays are among the best in America, you shouldn't be intimidated if your writing doesn't seem nearly so brilliant. (Our essays didn't make the book, either.) Some of these pieces are beautifully written, some are a bit awkward, but each gives a tiny flash into the lives of 50 ordinary students much like yourself. Each essay tells you something about its author that you wouldn't learn from reading grade transcripts and lists of extracurricular activities.

To be sure, many of the essays are "self-serving." They describe high school achievements and try to reinforce the rest of the application. But each piece also brings a special focus to the personality and mind of the writer, and that's exactly what admissions officers want to see.

Every college application that we have seen has plenty of space for you to list your grades and all your accomplishments. But the essay is the only section where you have total control. Your grades, your scores, your activities—they're history, and there is nothing you can do about them when you sit down to fill in the blanks. The essay, however, offers a precious opportunity for you to express your individuality, so don't squander the chance by just repeating what the rest of the application already shows. The essay is your chance to say, "Hey, *this* is me! I'm creative/witty/insecure/perceptive/enthusiastic/shy/adventurous—and all of the above."

The admissions officer wants to know the real you, and what makes you tick. What do you see differently from your friends? Why do you want to go to college? Do you talk to yourself? Hate sunny days? Take baths instead of showers? Still forget when to use "whom"? You don't have to vacation in the Orient or ski in the Olympics to have an amusing or interesting perspective. Some of the best essays are about seemingly trivial things, like Oreo cookies and babysitting. By finding the profound in the mundane, a writer can tell the admissions officer more about his personality than all the teacher references ever could.

So consider what you do each day, what you want, what you notice. The perfect essay may not pop into your head immediately, and you may have to write quite a few drafts before it clicks. But writing a good essay can make you think about the Meaning of Life, or about the junk accumulating under your bed. It can be illuminating, it can be fun, and it might even get you in.

Before You Start to Write

1. Begin thinking of essay topics early in the fall.

2. Write a time-line of your life, noting special dates and important events.

3. Make a list of five or six possible essay topics and discuss them with your friends, parents, teachers, etc.

4. Find a quiet place, and "write" the essay in your mind.

5. Everyone procrastinates to some extent. Be sure to give yourself plenty of time to work on the essay before the deadline.

An Interview
With an Admissions Officer

He still had a hundred essays to read before 6:00 p.m., and he was beginning to grow tired. My interview with him would offer a brief break from the Herculean task of narrowing 10,000 applicants to a freshman class of 900.

"I hope your book works," he joked, "so maybe next year I won't have to read 500 essays about the year-long drama of being student council president. I'm sorry, but successful car washes just don't make for enthralling reading."

I smiled. He rubbed his eyes.

"On a Wednesday in the middle of March this job gets tough. Sometimes it seems that there are only four types of essays: the 'class-president' essay, the 'I-lost-but-learned' sports essay, the 'I-went-to-Europe-and-learned-how-complex-the-world-is' essay, and the good old 'being-yearbook-editor-sure-is-hard-work' essay. When I read one of those, it takes amazing willpower to get to the third paragraph."

"So sometimes you don't read the whole essay?" I asked.

"No comment," he replied, changing the subject. "I wish students would realize that when they write they should have something to say. They should try to present their values and priorities by writing on a subject that really means something to them, because, other than the essay, all I have is a bunch of test scores and activities: 10,000 sets of numbers and facts. I'd like to be able to see beyond that. I want to see what makes someone tick."

"But couldn't that be dangerous?" I asked. "What if someone writes something really bizzare, just to avoid being 'boring'? Can strange ideas or comments hurt an applicant?"

"Well, if someone expressed homocidal tendencies, it would probably have a negative effect. Still, you'd be surprised how tolerant we are. A few years ago, we had a kid from Palestine apply. In his essay, he endorsed Yassir Arafat and the PLO. As far as he was concerned, Israel had usurped the rightful land of his people and should be treated as a criminal state. The admissions officer who covered the Middle East was an Orthodox Jew. Not only did the student get in, but he graduated with honors in political science.

"In fact, being off-beat or daring is usually a plus, as long as the student stays in control of his writing. The essays which are most effective seize a topic with confidence and imagination. Too many applicants treat their essay like a minefield. They walk around on tip-toes, avoiding anything controversial. Of course, the essay comes out two-dimensional, flat, and boring. It seems like many essays have been read, proof-read, and re-proof-read until all the life has been sucked out. I wish kids would just relax and not try to guess what the admissions committee is looking for. As soon as they start playing that game, they're going to lose. The essay won't be from the heart, and it won't work.

"The great essays—good writers discussing something of personal importance—stick out like diamonds in a coal bin. When we're sorting through the last few hundred applications, an essay that sticks out in an admissions officer's mind has got to help the applicant who wrote it."

"How important is it to be a good writer?" I asked.

"Writing style tells you a lot about the way a person thinks. I like when a student brings a sense of style to a piece, as a good essayist or editorial writer would do. I've always advocated reading the essays of E. B. White as a means of preparing for writing the essay. I also suggest that students read the editorial pages of the local newspaper. But we never discount the student who writes a simple, even awkward, essay which is sincere and moving.

"That's why I urge students to write as they would in a diary or a letter to a friend. When you write a letter, you may ramble, but when you're finished your letter sounds like something you would really say."

"So an honest, personal essay is best?"

"No, there is no 'best' type of essay. But when a 'personal' essay is done well, it can be very effective. The best I've ever read was written about 15 years ago by a football recruit. His application was perfect: high-school All-America quarterback, president of his class, 3.8 GPA, and a mile-long list of extra-curriculars. But his essay was about his stuttering. He wrote about his loneliness in junior high, about the girls who laughed at him, and about the wall he built around himself. Since football was something he really loved, he buried himself in it, spending afternoons in the weight room and on the track and nights in front of a mirror, practicing words and signals so he wouldn't embarrass himself by stuttering on the field.

"When you put an essay like that beside one of those self-absorbed recitals of high school achievements—there's just no comparison."

I decided to change the subject a little. "What really irritates you in an essay?"

"Arrogance and pretentiousness are bad, but the only thing that really bugs me is when a student doesn't put his personality into an essay. I always hear parents and students complain that colleges don't look so much at the individual student as they do at scores, grades, and class rank, so I'm disappointed when students don't take advantage of the only place in the application that allows them to express their individuality."

"Okay, then," I asked, "what do you really like to see?"

"I always enjoy essays where the author realizes that he's writing for an audience of real human beings. I also like essays with a touch of excitement and enthusiasm, and I like an applicant who demonstrates the ability to look at himself from the outside. And, of course, wit never hurts."

"So should applicants try to write funny essays?"

" 'Funny' isn't a good word, because there's a fine line between something that is humorous and something that is obnoxious or inappropriate. I much prefer an essay that is amusing because of its insight over one in which a kid is trying to write a string of one-liners—that rarely works."

I paused for a moment, thinking how to word my next question tactfully. "How much of a 'sell' is expected?"

"How much do I expect? Tons. I expect that most kids will try to wow me with their accomplishments, even though I could just look at their activities list if I really want to know. Each year, we have enough valedictorians, class presidents, and team captains to fill our freshman class five times. With that many talented kids, it's hard to impress me by listing your glorious achievements.

"How much of a 'sell' would I like? None. We enroll people, not cars, and I want more than a list of 'added features.' I am less interested in hearing what a student has done than hearing *why* he does what he does. Anything that comes across as a 'sell' is negative. If what comes through is a healthy self-confidence in your own accomplishments, then that's positive.

"Also, of course, a hard 'sell' can really backfire if the essay is not consistent with the rest of the application. A student once wrote an angry essay about social injustice and how the world should feed and clothe the poor. So I checked her list of activities. She had never been involved in any charities or community service programs, so I was pretty skeptical of her true feelings. No one likes hypocrisy, so if an applicant's record doesn't back up the essay, it can add a large negative factor into my decision."

"A common theme which is both uninteresting and unrevealing is participation in organizations which are 'in' at the time, such as SADD and SafeRides. Also, stating that you were listed in *Who's Who of American High School Seniors* only tells me that you were willing to pay."

I decided to go for all the marbles. "All said, what is the best essay?"

"What works the best? Honesty, brevity, risk-taking, self-revelation, imaginativeness, and fine writing: many of the attributes which are edited-out when you ask someone's opinion of your college essay. If a student reads his application before mailing it and can say 'this sounds like me,' then he's probably written the best essay possible. Students should feel more comfortable trusting their instincts. Nine times out of ten, an essay that feels good to the writer will be good for the reader too. And that should make the process better for all those involved— as essay writers or essay readers!"

(The quotes from the "admissions officer" above were compiled from the comments of all the admissions officers we interviewed.)

The Essays

For organizational purposes, we divided the essays into seven groups: Essays About the Application Process, Self-Description Essays, Realization Essays, Off-Beat Essays, Thought Essays, Activities Essays. and Descriptive Essays. Please bear in mind that this grouping is completely artificial. You don't have to write an essay that would fit neatly into one of these catagories.

We created the introductions to each group of essays from the comments submitted by admissions officers about the essays they sent. As well as being a fine piece of writing on its own, an essay might also exemplify a "type." For example, the piece about an inchworm by Jamie Mayer is a good example of the "Thought" essay. So, if you are going to write this type of essay, pay particular attention to the comments in the introduction, as well as to the styling of the essay.

Of course, the essay question may limit your range of responses. Most colleges have a vague, open-ended topic, like "Write a brief essay that in some way describes who you are." For that, you could write about practically anything. Other schools have questions that are more specific, like "Which adjective would describe you by those who know you best?" or even, "If you could have dinner with one famous person, who would it be and why?" Though answers to topics like these must be tightly structured, they still offer you the chance to develop a unique and memorable image.

The essays are reproduced exactly as they were submitted, though of course the typeface and spacing are different. (Also, a couple were handwritten.) We did not correct punctuation, spelling, or grammar errors in the essays. But note that very rarely would such correction be needed.

Finally, a warning. We know that no one would be foolish enough to copy any of these essays verbatim. However, we realize that some readers might be tempted to take one of these essays and "change it around" to suit his application. We hope you know how stupid that would be. For one thing, stealing an idea from an essay in this book or "paraphrasing" it would be dishonest. For another thing, it would severely jeopardize your chance of getting into college. Most admissions officers have read this book, and none would ever admit a plagiarist.

The following pages demonstrate the creative potential of the college application essay. We hope they will give you the confidence to write a bold, personal piece that will help an admissions officer see why you're special. Enjoy these essays, study them, and let them be a catalyst for your own creativity.

Essays About the Application Process

We all love to read about ourselves, so it should come as no surprise that a lot of college admissions officers recommended essays that were about—you guessed it—college admissions.

The first essay, *The Admissions Officer*, was probably most successful when read at 3:00 a.m., when the officer could identify with the blue-faced man paging through stacks of paper. A poem like this could offer an amusing break to the reader, but it is a gimmick, and gimmicks can be a substitute for real effort. They should be used with caution.

The Epistle of St. Geoff to Oberlin was both whimsical and intellectual. "I have to believe that the student was not only a good scholar of the gospels, but also had a great time writing this," the admissions officer noted. "You'll notice that this essay really doesn't discuss the student at all. It is so clever and amusingly written, however, that from it one cannot help but draw the conclusion that that the student is a witty and easy-going person who chose to poke fun at the college admissions process rather than become anxious about it. On the other hand, he avoids falling into the trap of stringing together a bunch of one-liners, as some students do, in the hope that we'll find him funny. A student who is naturally witty can write a witty essay. A student whose temperament is not so inclined often comes off like a cheap nightclub act when he or she attempts to amuse admission officers."

Unless you, too, are a naturally witty scholar, you probably should consider discussing yourself more directly. A wonderful example is Marjorie Just's piece about writing an essay. One admissions officer declared it her all-time favorite. "Like the others, this is craftily written, but it is uniquely successful in engaging the reader and conveying what the writer is like. I love the fairly easy-going self-consciousness of the essay as it describes not only the anxiety of essay writing for college applications themselves, but also her feelings about herself and her family."

If your point is valid, don't worry about pulling punches. Most officers we talked with would rather be offended than bored. Maria Guglielmo goes for the jugular when she makes fun of the massive amounts of paper generated by admissions offices, including her hopeful, Yale. In the next essay, Nicholas Cooper gambles by poking fun at Georgetown, Harvard, and Brown.

Ingrid Marie Geerken misspelled "Hemingway"—the type of gaffe that can really hurt if your application is assigned to a stickler for detail—but Ingrid's essay is so witty and creative that the University of North Carolina saved it as one of their favorites.

The final essays in this section openly break the rules set by some college admissions experts who have come up with an "infallible method" of essay writing, one we hope to dispel.

Eric Blum

Here is a sample of my poetry, in honor of the most dedicated college official:

The Admissions Officer

It is now three a.m.
　　and his eyes are getting glassy.
He sifts through wads of paper
　　watching reruns of Star Trek and Lassie.

His nasal drip is flaring up,
　　and his eyes are merely slits,
Liquid paper on the application forms
　　gives him endless fits.

Still he slaves into the night;
　　working countless hours,
To wake him up from this deep sleep
　　will take 300 showers.

His face is red, his tongue is dead
　　as if they've been doused in lava,
He burns his hand as he lunges for
　　his 6000th cup of Java.

His body's numb, his foot's asleep,
　　his only partner is caffine.
He thinks, "Any thing is better than this,
　　even swimming in a latrine!"

Who is this man so devoted
  that he'll never quit his job,
He'll die trying to combat
  the enormous paper blob?

Be thankful my friends that this man
  is not me or you;
He is the dedicated admissions officer,
  and his face is turning blue.

He works his magic for endless weeks,
  and his decision is always right,
Hmm, the kid has six fails,
  but his football's out of sight.

And so ends the tragic tale
  of a hard working, brilliant mind,
The next time you're turned down at school,
  please, please try to be kind.

This was a tribute to the little man
  the man who's brain must feel like lead,
I hope the man who admits me
  will someday sleep in bed.

Epistle of St. Geoff to Oberlin (regarding College Admissions)

Chapter 1
1 To all the beloved and
elect at Oberlin College.
2 Dearly beloved, I hope
above all things that thou
wouldst prosper and be in
good GPA standing.
3 Man is not to live by grades
alone but every score that
proceedeth out of Princeton,
New Jersey.
4 Eyes have not seen, nor
ears heard, neither has en-
tered into the heart of
man all the necessary calculus formulae.
5 Seek ye first the honor
roll and the 1400 range and
scholarships may be added into
you.
6 Render unto Caesar what
belongs to him and at least
you can mark it on the FAF.
7 Our Educational Testing
Service who art in New Jersey,
hallowed be thy scores.
8 Thy results come (no A.P.
1's) on earth as it is in New
Jersey.

9 For thine is the percentiles
and the selection indexes, and
the SDQ's and the FAF's, and
the TOEFL's, and the AP's, and
the NMSQQT's, and the et ceteras,
forever. Amen.
10 Judge not lest ye be considered
admissions staff material.
11 And why beholdest thou the
typo that is in thy brother's
application, but considerest not
the lousy penmanship that is in thine
own?
12 Blessed are they which apply,
perdaventure they they will get
lucky.
13 Blessed are they which are
accepted for they already got
lucky.
14 Blessed are the admission
counselors, albeit I know not
why.
15 In the beginning God created
the heaven and the earth.
16 On the eigth day God created
the college application which
just goes to show what working
overtime can do to someone.
17 Thou shalt have no other
colleges before me.
18 Remember the application
deadline day to keep it holy.
19 Six hours the night before shalt thou labour,
and do all thy work.
20 Honour thy father and thy
mother: especially if you
are a lagacy student.
21 Thou shalt not covet thy
neighbor's transcript, nor his
essays, nor his scholarship, nor
any thing that is thy neighbor's.

22 And woe unto them that are
with child, and to that
give suck in those days!
23 For then shall be great
tribulation, such as was
not since the beginning of the
world to this time, no, nor ever
shall be.
24 And except those days
should be shortened, there
should no flesh be saved.
25 For there shall be wailing
and gnashing of teeth.
26 Woe to the inhabiters of
the earth and of the sea!
27 And the heaven departed
as a scroll when it is rolled together; and every mountain
and island were moved out of
their places.
28 But relax, for soon the time
of tribulation shalt be passed,
and thou shalt go to thy mailbox
and find out how the tribunal hast
ruled.

Marjorie Just

I paused for a moment, staring at the paper. Hoo, I thought, I think I've read this question a hundred times and I still hyperventilate. What can I tell them that the rest of my application can't? I'm nice. I'm funny. I can be really damn funny when I want to be . . . I care a lot about my friends. And about my family. And I can do a few impressions when I act like a ham. But I can't say this stuff in an essay. It's not original, eyecatching, or witty. I can't be funny by trying really hard. No, funny is out. Don't even try it. It won't work. The college counselor said to be original and not just to summarize a trip you took. That would be a disaster because the admissions people read hundreds of them.

I heard my father coming up the steps. I knew it was Dad because every night around 9:00 he would trudge up the stairs. And before he got ready for bed, he would either ask me to do him a favor or he would go into each room on that floor and see how the room was doing. I knew he was doing the second because he always went to my brother's room first and he was in there now.

"How we doing, Tom?" he said.

"Fine."

"Let's go over the Latin vocabulary together."

"Dad, I'm doing science right now, all-right?"

He closed Tom's door. Here we go, I thought.

He opened the door and leaned into the room. "How we doing?"

"Okay."

"Do you think you'll have some time this weekend to go over math with Tom?"

I thought about the last time I tried to help Tom with math. And the fight we had gotten into because he thought I was being bossy. And the time before that. And the fight we had gotten into then about the same thing. But I like math so

I said, "Sure," and hoped Tom would be in a better mood.

"Thanks," he said, "he really looks up to you. I know it's hard to tell sometimes because he's trying to be cool. But he cares about what you think so try not to be very critical."

I nodded. I don't know what he's talking about, I thought, I get the feeling he feels exactly the opposite.

"What are you doing?" he asked.

"I'm working on the essay."

"Oh," he said. Not a short "oh" of comprehension, but a long let-me-tell-you-what-I-think "oh."

Here it comes again, I thought.

"You know, you've had some unique experiences these past two summers, going to Finland and working in France."

Again I nodded. It was useless to tell him that it was a bad idea because he had a point to get across (even though it was the same point for the fifth time), and if I didn't let him finish completely, he would call me stubborn and start a fight. Or even worse, he would tell me that it was fine if I didn't want him to talk. He just wouldn't talk to me at all, then. Yes, Dad, say it, I thought, come on: "comparing the two trips would be interesting."

"Maybe you might like to compare the two trips. Talk about the differences between living with a French family and living with a Finnish family."

"Yeah. I'll think about it, Dad, but it has to be something original, not an 'I had a great vacation' thing."

"Yes," he said, "it's important to show that, just like any other seventeen year old, you have fears and insecurities. You're human for goodness sake . . . " He looked up at the ceiling for a moment.

Uh oh, I thought, it's acting time. He's pretending he's me writing the essay. God, he's so melodramatic.

" . . . In Finland, though I did not have the comfort of knowing the language, as I did in France, I felt much more secure in Finland, for I did not have any responsibility there. In France, however, I was in charge of a boy and a girl, being an au pair girl, and I had to give them a feeling of security while, at the same time, feeling insecure myself about the society."

I nodded. That's the stupidest, most infantile piece of crap I have ever heard, I thought, it also has about six conjunctions that don't belong, and is about as dull as a flat pancake. You really have no idea how I felt these past two summers, have you?

"Do you know what I mean?" he said. "Obviously, this is just a rough idea, but do you see what I mean?"

"Yeah. I'll try, Dad, but I'm not sure if I'll write about Finland or France."

"Well, I think it would be a good idea. They were both great experiences." He closed the door and went to his room.

I thought, it's amazing the non-conversations I have with him. I just nod and nod and pretend to agree. Everyone spoke English in Finland. I had no real problem with the language. And I worked in Finland every day in Mrs. Sillanpaa's store. I just never minded it.

I got up from my desk and went downstairs to the kitchen where my mom was grading papers.

"Hi, Mom."

"Hi, Honey. How are you doing?" I went over and gave her a hug. The nice thing about hugging my mom is that sometimes she needs it as much as I do.

"I don't know," I said, "I'm trying to write my essay and I don't really know what to write about. I want to write something good and revealing and all that."

"Well, how about the time in elementary school when you asked the teacher to give the girls equal time on the playing fields?"

"Mom, I was about nine years old and I don't remember it."

"Oh," she giggled. "How about Finland?"

"I don't know. I don't think it would be very good but Dad thinks it's a great idea. He even started acting it out, you know?"

She smiled. "He does like to do that .. But, Honey, you know you should only write what you feel comfortable with. Probably some experience where you learned something, but it doesn't have to be a big revelation."

Yeah, all-right. I get it. It's just kind of scary to start. But writing about Finland would just come out stupid."

"I don't think so," said my father, standing in the doorway of the kitchen. I quickly turned to face him.

"Dad, I thought you went to bed."

"Why don't you think you can write about Finland," he stated.

I knew he didn't think there was an answer, so he didn't bother to ask me. He just stated it. I shrugged my shoulder. "I just don't think it would tell enough about me personally. I mean, I had a lot of fun, but my personality didn't change or anything."

"Oh, Marjorie," he whined in his why-do-you-have-to-bug-me-with-this voice, "would you stop scholtzing around and write the goddamn essay on Finland?" When he said this, he did something that always scares me. While he was yelling, he first threw his hands in the air. Then he put his hands on both sides of his face which had turned red. Then he turned to me, bent over so his head was just over mine, and shook his hands, palms up, in front of my face when he said "Goddamn essay."

"Dad?" I said as loudly as he had. I took a step back and looked at my mom.

"Harold, let her write what she thinks is best."

"Marion." He gave her a familiar look that meant he didn't want to see his wife contradicting him.

"No, Hal, she's right. The admissions people don't want to hear a travellogue." My dad's eyes widened and his face turned a brighter shade of red. "She wants to write something more personal than that."

"I did not spend all that money sending her to Finland so she could write about something more personal!!"

"What?!" I was so surprised and angry I wanted to punch him. "What the hell are you talking about? I did not go to Finland so I would have something to write about! I went there and had a great time! It wasn't an educational ex-perience! And my Finnish family was so wonderful and loving that I didn't have any stupid insecurities about the society! But you don't know that because you never asked me how I felt there! You didn't! I can't believe it." I took a big breath and calmed down a little. "Dad. I'm going to write about my personality. I want to show them a little of myself, not my ac-complishments."

"I see your trip to Finland as something unique about yourself." I looked at the floor. There was no point arguing if he wasn't going to try to see my side.

I quietly said, "I'm not going to write about Finland and I'm not going to submit it for your approval. I appreciate your wanting to help me but I think I can and should speak for myself." I left the kitchen and went up to my room. I read the essay question and then began to write:

"I paused for a moment, staring at the paper. Hoo, I thought, I think I've read this question a hundred times and I still hyperventilate..."

Maria Guglielmo

Question: What weighs 18,370.49 grams, more or less, grows every day, and is in the process of swallowing my desk? Answer: The total amount of college-related literature I have received since my junior year in high school.

When I started gathering information concerning colleges, I really had no conception of the immense quantity of printed material, mostly unsolicited, that can be acquired by one individual without really trying. In my naivete, I assumed that the process of gathering information would be more akin to diving for pearls of knowledge than to being submerged in a sea of college catalogs. I didn't dislike the tidal wave of paper, but I also didn't expect it. After a while, it became a rather exciting experience. Perhaps being contacted by mail is an ego-gratifying event. There is something about large numbers of colleges sending one pamphlets and letters that causes a person to feel wanted.

After going to the trouble of saving these quantities of paper over a period of two years, and then weighing them to determine how much paper I actually had, I decided to determine some other useful information from my collection. True to my scientific background, I devised a unit of standard measure. Naturally, I selected the Yale *Bulletin* as the standard for college mailings, and found that it in itself has several interesting properties. It weighs roughly 226.8 grams, for one thing, and it has ninety-eight pages of about 337.5 square centimeters each.

I realize that the above facts may not seem earth-shattering. Einstein was misunderstood too! However, if the *Bulletin* is set up as a standard, it is possible to estimate the total area of all the college pamphlets and catalogs which I have collected. It comes out to the rather imposing sum of 2,679,074.9 square centimeters.

Having determined this fascinating information, I then

wondered a while about what possible significance my findings would have. After deep thought, I concluded that there wasn't any. I did determine, however, that this area, while less than a tenth of an acre by itself, was representative of all the potential acres of paper possessed by all the applicants to Yale. In fact, if Yale's campus were somehow to be flattened completely, it would only take 2,567.98 applicants with their college information to cover all one hundred and seventy acres of Yale. This number, as you are no doubt aware, is but a fraction of the total number of applicants to the university each year. It is well within the power of the total pool of applicants to cover Yale's campus several times over. I certainly would not want anyone to consider this as a potential hazard, or even as a remote possibility, but if I were in the vicinity and I espied a large group of steamrollers headed toward the campus, I would leave in a hurry.

There are other attendent dangers to this insidious accumulation of paper. If I were to continue to be an applicant for the rest of a lifetime, say sixty years, I would be swamped with over 54,600 grams of this material. Lest one shudder at the thought, be assured that I have no intention of remaining an applicant any longer than is absolutely necessary.

As a final note, I would like to add my best wishes toward the efforts in selecting a class to enter Yale. Since each application has an area of at least 7,095 square centimeters, your office will probably be receiving almost 84,182 square feet of paper forms this year. I hope that the office will find my 7,095 square centimeters to be on the crest of this tsunami of paper, and not in the trough.

Nicholas Cooper

Dorothy awoke when her house crash-landed. She stepped out to a world of greenery. At her feet were two wondrous slippers, fashioned of ivy.

As she put them on, she saw skate-board riders. "Where am I?" she asked.

"You are in the land of Odds. Each of us scored 800 on our S.A.T.'s."

"Congratulations. Verbal or math?"

"800 Combined. We didn't get into our safeties, so we just circle on on our boards. You can borrow mine."

Doing a graceful handstand as she skated, Dorothy looked up at a tall youth holding a basketball.

"I'm Scarecrow. I'm waiting for a talent scout."

"Why?"

"I need a basketball scholarship to go to Georgetown," said Scarecrow.

"Why can't you go without a scholarship?"

"I have no brain."

"Colleges won't want me either," said Dorothy. "How can I make my life seem eventful?"

"Just follow the Rhetoric Road to the Advisor of Odds," said Scarecrow, "I'd be pleased to show you the way."

Dorothy and Scarecrow followed the road but soon stopped to rest. A girl walked over and offered them water. "Who are you?" asked Dorothy.

"My name is Sterling. I'll be rejected because I can show no community service and have no heart. I'm afraid I'm metallic."

"We are soon to see an expert," said Scarecrow. "He can assay your composition and assess your essay."

Continuing, the three came upon a young man with long hair, wearing beads and peace patches, reclining on a couch.

"Welcome to my couch. My name is Dandelion."

"Why are you dawdling, Dan?" asked Scarecrow.

"I have no motivation."

"Motive enough to join us," said Scarecrow. All four proceeded, comparing their extra-curricular activities, until they finally reached the Advisor's office.

"Excuse me," said Dorothy. "We'd like to see the Advisor."

"I'm sorry," replied the Secretary. "You'll have to make an appointment. His next free is February 4."

"But that's too late for Rice! We're ruined."

Suddenly the Good Babe of the West Coast appeared. "Chill out," she said. "Scarecrow, you won't need brains if you take an S.A.T prep course. Sterling, don't worry; hearts hardly count. Dandelion, you are unlikely to work no matter where you go, but you would not be alone at Harvard. And now you, Dorothy. All along you have had the ivy slippers. Nothing can stand in your way. You are going to Brown!"

"Then why did we come all this way?" asked Dorothy.

"Oh, Dorothy, Dorothy! Life can't be completely fair! Competition has to cause unhappiness! There's too little room in the inn. But you had to find that out for yourself."

"You're right," said Dorothy. "Well, goodbye friends. I'll never forget you. There's no place like Brown . . . There's no place like Brown. . . "

Ingrid Marie Geerken

Once Upon a falling October, screechingly close to when all post secondary applications were due, a girl in red hightops, (preferring to write in the third person), sat down to explain who she was (who *was* she?) on a blank, square piece of paper. She thought (this was done with an alarming frequency) how she yearned to fling herself across that little, but, oh, so very demanding, white essay space, seal herself up snugly in a rectangular envelope—lift the gooey flap before it slammed shut, slide her arm out the back, and stamp it right in the corner. If her mom were home—she'd ask her politely to address the envelope and send it off to the **Undergraduate Admissions, Monogram Building 153-A, Country Club Road, Chapel Hill, N.C. 27514**.

On second thought (something she also had with an alarming frequency) she thought that writers are so temperamental that she would probably crumple up and throw herself away.

"Where are they when I need them!?", she cried in delirious desperation, groping for the heroes living on her shelves, lounging luxuriously inside her books, rooming comfortably with their settings, characters, plots, themes, styles, tones, ironies and symbolisms.

"Certainly their words chiseled a glimpse of human nature into a monument of truth. Surely, they could write a classic— but, the question is—could they write a college essay?"

If you wish, **use the following space to provide information about yourself which you think may help us in making our decision. Please add extra sheets if necessary.**

What would Hemmingway write? I mused.

My name is Ernest. I am a man. I am a writer. I would like to attend the University of North Carolina At Chapel Hill.

Presenting Faulkner.

The name given to me at the moment of glorious birth when the fruits of the conception that were created through the guiding hands of the most Holy Being through the act of ultimate love between those who gave me life is the striking and most beautiful appelate of William Faulkner.

e.e. cummings in the Spotlight:

mY (N)a(ME) !!! E.?e. (is)

sgnimmuC.

i a　　　　m. a

(poet.)(.)

i.

Though he claimed that brevity was the soul of wit, Shake-speare always had a way with words:

The wheel of fortune hath spun—that arrant whore bestowed upon me the most wretched of inquiries. Thy wit shall not go slipshod. Hear me committee—set less than thou trowest. I owest thou naught my name. Go to, have thy wisdom; it is William Shakespeare.

J.D. Salinger is a favorite of mine:

Damn it! Why the hell are you asking my name? Phonies are always asking crap like that. I don't know why, but they get a goddamn kick out of asking people who they are and what their names are and if they have a permanent mailing address. Those phony bastards really kill me. They want to know what you're goddamn address is so that they can send you a goddamn letter saying that you're not good enough for them. Things like that really depress me.

David Thoreau meditates:

Why I was named David Thoreau. With respectful civil disobedience, I must defer this question until I have gone into the woods and contemplated the matter more thoroughly. (thoreau-ly.) UNC. "There I might live, I said . . . "

Freud insists:

My identification is goal-oriented with a small tendency toward narcissism. My Id, Ego, and Superego are all fully developed and the most predominant defense mechanism of *my ego is projection. (For example, If I am not accepted into the University Of North Carolina At Chapel Hill, I will utilize my ability to blame it on outside or extenuating circumstances, and I will say,* They don't know a good essay when they see one.*) Because of my pleasure derived from relieving myself during the Anal stage of development, I am basically an outgoing person. I chew on my pen caps because some of my libido was stunted in the oral stage of development.*

Arthur Miller dramatizes:
BEN: *Why, boys, when I was seventeen I walked into the University of North Carolina at Chapel Hill and when I was twenty-one I walked out.* He laughs. *And by God I was wise!*
WILLY: *"You see what I been talking about? The greatest things can happen!"*

I say, (says she, switching from third to first person) that my name is Ingrid. I think too much, I laugh too loud, I live intensely. Heaven for me would to be locked up in a small room with stacks and piles and reams of blank paper; Hell for me would to be locked up in a small room with stacks and piles and reams of blank sheets of white paper, without a pencil, pen, typewriter, piece of chalk, crayon, carbon, paint, or any other type of writing utensil. It's equivalent to locking Michaelangelo up in a room with thousands of pure marble blocks and refusing to give him a chisel. (The situations are equivalent—not the artists.)

When I go to college, (Will UNC have anything to do with me?), I have decided that I will bring forth from my room these things: 1)The complete works of J.D. Salinger, 2)*A Separate Peace* by John Knowles, 3)*A Winters Tale* by Mark Helprin, 4)Poetry by Carl Sandburg and T.S. Eliot, 5)My poster of the statue of David by Michelangelo, 6)Mickey Mouse and my Teddy Bear, 6)My watercolors, 7)My Talking Heads Albums, 8)My newspapers, my yearbook (My unsigned yearbooks. I always hated signing them). 9)My English teacher's address. 10)Myself.

My name is Ingrid and more than anything else in the world right now, I want to become a part of the University of North Carolina at Chapel Hill.

(Name Withheld)

Recently, several authors of the college admissions process have outlined an infallible method which any student can use to write his way into the university of his choice. They claim that there are three general categories into which the student applicants can be divided, and that the best way for an applicant to decide what to emphasize in his essays is to determine whether he is an "outright brain", a "special talent" or your basic "all-American kid", and begin to write accordingly. What at first confused me, but now gives me a kind of secret pleasure, is that I am not convinced that I am any one of the above.

The fact is, when I see my friends babbling incoherently about some calculator-toting zombie with A's in six A.P. classes and test scores that read like the price of a 1986 Mercedes Benz, I am inclined to gossip with them. But then it occurs to me that I tend to place in the "brain" category too! I have no idea how it happened; I don't feel any smarter than anyone else. To me "brilliant" is the description of my friend who can brew home-made English beer, maintain an impressive G.P.A. and hit a volleyball over an eight foot net at a 60 degree angle. Needless to say, brewing English beer doesn't show up on the standard report card.

Meanwhile, I have a difficult time believing that I might be another "Alvin, the Colorful Bookworm" (God forbid!). For the most part, I think that the major difference between my peers and myself is that when they don't dig reading "Portrait of the Artist as a Young Man" the first time through, they have enough guts to toss James Joyce into the trash, whereas I, out of obstinacy and the blind conviction that classic literature is relevant, keep plugging away until everything is as clear as water. Every once in a while I wonder if I'm more pleased with myself or with Joyce, but after thirteen years of reading, I seem to have decided that books are a lot of fun. If this has anything to do with intelligence, I couldn't say.

Now I have to ask myself if I'm a "special talent" instead, but again I am stumped. I have to admit it: I simply have not subjected myself to learning the sitar. I can't even say that I can speak the ancient dialect of the Watusi Warriors. This is not to say that I can do nothing well. On the contrary, I'm not at all bad at a number of things, but I've never been able to drop one for the other. Thus, after a few years of competitive bicycling, I can ride over a 6000 foot pass with some of the best cyclists in California, but people who are "special talents" would cackle at my so-called skills. Even as far as writing goes, "Rolling Stone" isn't exactly dying to acquire my services. Basically, I have been happy knowing that if I really want to build prize-winning sand castles or be a French chef, I probably can, but as yet I haven't felt pressed to make that kind of decision.

If I am neither a brain not an expert piano player, according to the authorities I must be the "all-American" boy next door type. This is fine with me just as long as his idea of fun is being kidnapped by an outlaw motorcycle gang, taken to the Mojave and having Welsh ale poured down his throat. Though I wouldn't discourage the pursuits of others, I am not very comfortable with baseball, Christmas carols, the Boy Scouts or some of the other things typical young people are supposed to enjoy.

On the other hand, maybe I am a bit ordinary. I hang around with the average contradictory beach-oriented crowd . . . with people who pity hippies but look up to G. Gordon Liddy, with people whose feelings about war are as uncertain as those about their future, whose catchwords include "iconclast", "goon", and all forms of "to excite", who are anti-religion, anti-fanatic, and anti-love, but definitely pro-life, who are both for and against Armageddon.

In short, I am one of those people who pretend to be evasive but who are actually strongly attracted to everything in a secret, special way. What I don't know is why there is not a category for satirists.

Michael D. Schill

Michael D. Schill
by Michael D Schill

Hmm... Mr. Schill ~ it says here that you "want to enter Davidson as soon as possible" in order to "finally start getting an education." Would you care to elaborate on this?

Yes; what I mean is that I find my high school work not at all challenging and that...

I don't get enough stimulation for intellectual and creative growth. I get a lot of stimulation from my friends and the people I associate with, and I do a lot of thought on the side, but school just doesn't seem to give me much. From what I hear of Davidson, I would be involved in in-class discussion and other things that would present different perspectives of ideas and problems of mankind.

What's this about "thought on the side" and "different perspectives"? Don't you want to learn what you're being taught?

Oh, let's not be so naive. Nothing worth learning can be taught. It can be introduced, and insight can be offered on it, but it has to be learned on one's own. A student is going to learn only as much as he wants to.

And how much do you want to learn, Mr. Schill? And why?

Ahhh... Now that's the central point of life. My life, anyway. The search for knowledge. With knowledge of the past one can understand what is going on in the world now. One can apply knowledge from one situation to another to gain a new perspective on it. And once one has this knowledge, one can begin to make connections — cause and effect, parallels, and others — between events, philosophies, and viewpoints. Once one has made these connections, one can begin to interpret things in one's own way. That's what I want to do — to interpret things artistically. To see their artistic value and bring it out;

to incorporate that knowledge into my art. That, too, is the purpose of Art: to offer new perspectives.

So you're saying that you want to become an artist to help other people gain insight on the human condition?

Well, I'm certainly not in it for the money. Yes, to answer you more directly. That's what Literature and Art are about; they are creative comments on life. I want to use my artistic talent, to put some knowledge and...

...insight back **into** the system. To teach people, to stamp out ignorance. Ignorance is one of the few things I really hate. If one could supplant ignorance with understanding, one could completely decimate prejudice, fear, East-West tensions — almost all conflicts that exist.

That's an impossibility.

Maybe. However, one has to try, right?

You seem very casual about the whole thing; very flip and informal. Don't you consider this important?

I'm not trying to be flip, and I do feel that these things of which we speak are of **basic** importance to mankind; they are solid things to build on. I'm just looking to learn something — don't you believe that one can learn and have fun learning?

Well, I ... suppose so...

And since these things — Knowledge, Art, Literature, Thought — are, or should be, common to all men, don't you think that being "casual" and "informal" at the right times can get a point across?

I suppose you're right.

Did I get my point across?

I think so. Good luck in your search for knowledge.

Will Michael D. Schill beat the evil force of Competition? and get in to Davidson? Find out next issue!

MDS

40

While You're Writing

1. Make sure you are answering the question appropriately.

2. Have a dictionary, a thesaurus, and a bottle of "white-out" handy.

3. Try different atmospheres. Write in silence, with music, at a baseball game, even during a boring math class.

4. If you get "writer's block," first try writing the whole essay the way you would say it. Or, "talk" the essay into a tape recorder. Lastly, try stream-of-consciousness writing: write whatever you're thinking, and don't let your pencil leave the page for two minutes.

5. Let your essay sit for a few days, then re-read it. You'll probably find a number of improvements you can make.

The Self-Description Essay

All essays describe the applicant, but some do it more bluntly than others. Often, the application asks you pointedly to "discuss yourself" or "tell us more about yourself than your transcripts and scores already have." Stanford, for example, asks applicants to describe themselves using a "single adjective."

It's usually easy to write about yourself. High school students especially are experiencing a wealth of self-revelation, so topics aren't hard to find. What's tough is making your writing interesting and memorable. After all, how many essays that begin "I've recently learned how important my friends are to me" or "After years of arguing, my parents and I are finally starting to develop a better relationship" do you think one poor admissions officer can take?

The first essay of this group, written by Dylan Tweney, describes a young man brimming with excitement and potential. "This essay blew me away, and still does," wrote Evelyn Stockton Layne of the Williams College admissions office. "It offers such a direct view into the contradictions and complexities of a highly imaginative, creative, and complex person. It is both bold and sensitive, amazingly rich in imagery and unusual in structure. Dylan is a good bet to be a mold-breaker, innovator—a shaping force—no matter what field he eventually reunites flesh and skeleton in pursuit of." To anyone who doubts the importance of the application essay, imagine Ms. Layne rooting for you like that in an admissions conference!

On Melinda Menzer's essay about telekenesis, ketchup soup, and searching for truth, the admissions officer said, "You have to believe that Melinda will make the tissue box move. She manages to wrap up teddy bears, *Crime and Punishment*, cookies, and nuclear holocaust into an utterly convincing essay. She sweeps you away with the power of her ambition and positive thinking. Wouldn't you love to have her as a roommate?"

The third essay is good for anyone who has ever said to himself, "But I'm so ordinary. Nothing has ever happened to me that's worth writing about." The admissions officer explained that this writer "has a knack for providing images which clarify his main point—that one does not have to be a standout or famous to be important. I suspect that few students could write an essay with this kind of skill and creativity. However, what most students can draw from it is how a single, striking image or a series of analogies can have the impact that more formal prose can sometimes lack."

Sarah Chinn's essay is yet another example of someone who can laugh at her town, her religion, and herself, while still maintaining an enthusiastic level of energy that shines through.

When Stanford asks students to describe themselves in a single word and to follow with explanation, many applicants try to be clever, writing simply "concise" or "brief," and then leaving the rest of the page blank. This ploy almost never works, but avoiding gimmicks doesn't mean you have to play by the rules. In writing her "sporglandish" essay, Adrienne Greaves makes up her own word. She's breaking the rules, but who cares? Her essay is entertaining and honest. The next piece, also for Stanford, is a little more conventional, but it expresses the factors which shape the author's life with wit and warmth. And Michael Meusey, in a quest for three descriptive adjectives, creates a relaxed, playful essay. He seems to have had fun writing his piece, and that alone says a lot about his personality.

The most effective writers don't tell you they are funny, warm, and distinctive, they show you. Karen Duffy and Christa Hershman describe themselves in a style that strings together unrelated images which, when taken as a whole, represent dynamic individuals.

Dylan Tweney

I am:

Blinded by science, saved by Zero, thrown from a fairy tale, across the pit of what could be, and back into the magic again, smoking with restrained passion and still shivering from the bitter winds that blow through my skeleton, which I left behind for awhile when I decided that I was a magic soul trapped in a mechanistic body.

The funniest thing is that my skeleton does just as well by itself as it did when fleshed and blooded and clothed. No one has noticed that my devotion and greatest concentration are no longer on my schoolwork, even while that bare skeleton of attention is beginning to crumble.

I am:

Old like Kronos, young as the dew, day-to-day variable like the wind, now a soaring dove far above the petty concerns of familial and social life, now an irascible, excitable bear in a box. Obviously egotistical as hell. I've always been plagued with fantasies of greatness. They're fine, but at one time they were the only fantasies I had. Eager to be the greatest scientist the world had ever known, I devoted myself to my studies and launched myself into the sea I thought I belonged in, because I had known no other since falling in love with school at the age of five. I've since re-emerged from that surf, foam on my mouth.

But to many I seem stable, calm, rational, "boring." They may be right. It's possible that I'm suffering from delusions of artistic grandeur, or that I'm simply trying to make myself feel better by pretending to be of a romantic cut. Or it may be that I actually am a turbulent person with a calm exterior deriving from a strong sense of self-control and modesty. I can truly let go to create and to communicate only in art (but what a term— "art" —it sounds like some kind of prostitution). So my soft artist's body: blood, brain, intestines and all, has gone on to paint, draw, write (and sing surreptitiously—and quite poorly—in the closet), while my bones remain behind to prop up a convenient image back in school.

I am also:

Obsessed. The hormonal soup and budding sexual instinct present in every seventeen-year-old boy happened to swirl up into the head of one whose patience, dedication, faithfulness, and general stupidity amaze even himself. That is to say (with all the irony due such a bizarre Junior year): I spent almost an entire year and a half waiting, admiring, and damn near privately worshipping a young lady with whom I was desperately infatuated; by the time she came around last summer and decided that she was crazy about me, too, it was two weeks before she had to leave for Germany as an exchange student—meaning I have to wait another year, for no certain return. But, I love her, quite sincerely, and my feeling is that most people really love only a few times in their lives, so I'm not giving up on this one, not yet, not just because over five thousand miles and thirty million seconds separate us.

I am:

Emerging from this essay intact, shaking off the beads of fancy and words and metaphor, hair dripping with sweat from the exertion of the usual Olympian attempt to create (100% self) and communicate (half self and half audience), yielding one more work with the ideal ratio of 3 me : 1 you. Another four-part structure! If I'm done writing, you're done reading me. Do you feel you know me any better?

"Life is serious but art is fun." —John Irving

Melinda Menzer

Sometimes I sit in my room and try to move things. I stare as hard as I can at, say, a tissue box and think, "MOVE!" Crinkling up my forehead, scrunching up my eyes, I will with all might that the tissue box will levitate. So far, nothing has ever moved. But I am still hoping to develop extra-sensory powers.

I guess what I fear most is being ordinary. Well, let me qualify that. I fear nuclear holocaust, robbers under the bed, big, furry tarantulas, and the theft of my dear teddy bear, Phoebe, just as much or more. But I don't want to be ordinary. Ordinary is boring; ordinary is pointless; ordinary is so very . . . ordinary. Anyone can be ordinary. But I don't want to be just anyone.

Reading *Crime and Punishment* made me think about being ordinary. Raskolnikov, the main character, wants to prove that he is extraordinary, that he is a super-man. To do this, he kills a woman pawnbroker. Now, I don't need to kill anybody; I am a tad more laid back than Raskolnikov. But I, too, want to do something. I have a predilection towards living in a garret, eating ketchup soup and Saltines, writing the The Great American Novel. Or, like Larry Darrell in *The Razor's Edge*, I could travel the world in search of truth, doing good "for the love of a God he doesn't believe In." I want to sacrifice for a worthy cause; I want to change the world; I want to make the difference.

Now, they tell me I'm a pretty smart cookie. I have the credentials: good SAT scores, National Merit Semifinalist, four AP classes. As cookies go, I'm near the top of the jar. But am I a boring, bland, sugar cookie or an ordinary, carbon copy, buy-at-the-supermarket cookie? Or am I a super-duper, slightly eccentric, rough but delicious, homemade, one-of-a-kind oatmeal-raisin cookie? I refuse to be just another ordinary cookie in the crowd. Eventually I'll win the Nobel Prize for Literature, or I'll discover the nature of genetic processes. Perhaps tomorrow will be the day I make the tissue box move.

(Name Withheld)

Who is (Name Withheld)? Good question.

I am a familiar person, one that you have certainly seen before. I am an old acquaintance who I'm sure you know quite well. You see, when all is said and done and everyone has gone home to sleep, I stand there alone; noble and unnoticed. I observe it all. I am the hero's best friend.

It seems that it has always been my part in life to be the second man on the moon or the guy who blocked for O.J. Simpson. I'm not complaining though. My job is very important and in many ways, much more difficult. I have to be brilliantly consistent without ever being obtrusive. For example: I'm the blond-haired kid who gets hit by a ricochet just as the army is about to go over the top. My dying words are "tell my mother I fought bravely". I'm just a sweet, simple kid who doesn't deserve to die in absolutely every war movie you have ever seen. It's the kind of consistency that requires a very light hand; *anyone* could be John Wayne.

In a world of "stars", "co-stars" and "special guest stars", I'm a "with"; but I always remember my lines and play my character to its fullest. All I ask is that you be patient and attentive, allow me to make you laugh or cry. Let me do this and we will both be happy. I guarantee it.

I'm the person who places the parsley on your $17.50 Veal Oscar. I never use too much or too little and my little piece of parsley adds style, grace and beauty to your dining experience. Without my parsley you would detect a vital missing ingredient but would be hard pressed to figure out exactly what it is. You'd inspect the wine and perhaps lightly pepper your food, yet something would be missing. Everyone needs a little parsley.

Finally, I'm that third person singular narrator that you've been wondering about all these years. For as long as you've been reading books, you've been wondering who the omniscient observer is. We are one in the same. I know all, and what I don't know I can find out or, best of all, make up. I can wield my imagination as a sword or a feather; sometimes both.

I like being the hero's best friend even if it does occasionally mean being Andrew Jackson's horse or the Habsburg's butler. Though you may not remember my name, you will never forget me. You will miss me when I have gone.

Sarah Chinn

Most people are afraid of what will happen on Judgement Day, but I don't have to worry about it. I'll walk into a room, my karma floating gently before me, arguing with my eternal soul about who should go in front, and a great voice will boom:

"Will the real Sara Chinn please stand up!" And there I shall be, facing the void between heaven and hell (purgatory is not a Jewish fear; we work off our guilt on Earth) not knowing where to put myself. Let me explain.

I am a "little bundle of contradictions". I live my life between the one hand and the other, weighing up the odds and waiting for it to come out even. I am happy to be alive, joyous, outgoing, loving and lovable. On the other hand, I am sometimes deeply depressed, afraid, shy, hating and hateful, disillusioned with the world as it is and wishing how it might be. I am a city girl: I love noise, buildings, even dirt, and the never ending grimy rain. But there is a freedom in endless miles of green field that draws my head away from the grubby claustrophobia of New York City and its concrete mile-high gravestones, stretching out into one enormous mausoleum. I am typical prim English, the product of a girls' school education: dogmatic, self-assured, liberated but restrained. And then I am the American High School Senior: wild, laughing at fast cars and football games, madly applying to college, going out to parties and burning the candle at both ends, never fearing the dripping wax as it gets nearer and nearer the middle.

You're right, scores and grades can tell you very little about a person, although it is difficult to sum up "everything-about-you-we-don't-already-know-but-you-think-is-interesting" in such a small space. I am glad that Yale is not the Eternal Judge, although at the moment it feels that way. But the real Sarah Chinn...? The real Sarah Chinn loves her life, loves her inconsistencies, loves to make people wonder what she will do next. She is a little radical in her politics, a little hypocritical in her actions. She is trying to change the world and trying to stop it from changing her too much.

Adrienne Greaves

I am very "sporglandish," which I will now define. Sporg-landish means rather shy around new people in new situations, but funloving and daring with friends. A sporglandish person likes to be with people, talking and laughing with a sibling un-til the wee hours, but she needs to retreat occasionally to sit alone and ponder, or dance an encore for an imaginary crowd. Such a word describes someone who loves the outdoors and willingly wades knee-deep in mud to catch a frog or cater-pillar, but also enjoys splurging for a high-fashion magazine and imagining herself a French model in outlandish clothes before a flood of buyers and photographers. Sporglandish peo-ple are generally bleeding-hearts, the kind who have trouble killing ants and want to grow up to be veterinarians.

I am sorry I could not give you a more conventional adjec-tive. "Content" or "satisfied" sounded too complacent, and "creative" seemed too much of a compliment. "Individual-istic" came the closest, but I think you know me better now, even if I had to create a word to tell you.

(Name Withheld)

In the sense of out-of-fashion and out-of-date, I am obsolete. In a world of career orientation and pre-professional specialization, I am a voracious educational omnivore, left in the dust.

I do admire those galloping ahead of me on the straight and narrow path. Unfortunately, I am doomed to see eighteen solutions to every problem, six sides to every square and often analyze myself into a ditch.

Yet, I do not lack for company on the wayside. The reasonings that plague me are in great demand among my friends. When x is inexplicably furious with y, I can insure that claws remain retracted, and often squander soothing words and a hug or two even when peace reigns.

Although my own future is far from clear, I try to avoid short-sightedness. I read beyond the trendy headlines of the newspapers proclaiming new patriotism and prosperity. Before finishing my morning coffee, I actually turn the page and worry.

Worrying, of course, is no end to itself. To combat a tendency to despair, I want to have all the tools necessary to help solve problems. I want to absorb as many different perspectives, thoughts and languages as possible. Despite this stigma of obsolescence, I am determined to make myself useful one day.

Michael Meusey

I would like to take this opportunity to discuss the experience I had filling out this application. In particular, I will focus on the section which asks for three adjectives to describe oneself. I found this to be a somewhat difficult task, having to sum myself up in three words. In this essay I will relate to you the trials and tribulations of my attempt to do so.

At first it seemed this would be the easiest part of the application. When I first read it the three words that immediately came to mind to describe myself perfectly were: tall, dark and handsome. However, when I sprung this idea on my girlfriend I began to have second thoughts. First of all she said that I wasn't really tall, just above average in height. Also, the only time I could be considered dark was at the height of my summer tan, and even that was stretching it. Finally, she didn't know if she would go so far as handsome, but she did say that I was not ugly. At that point I decided to revise my choices since "above average height, occasionally dark, and not ugly" wasn't exactly the image I wanted to give.

I was then struck by a new inspiration. I could use words that were very vague and able to be interpreted in several different ways. I thought of such words as "talented", "determined", and "motivated." I figured I was home free since these words would make me sound good and I wouldn't have to say where my talent, determination and motivation lie, it would just be assumed I was referring to academics. As I went to type them onto the application form, the pat on the back I was giving myself became a slap in the face when I discovered I had to explain why I had chosen those words. So much for that idea.

My next approach was to portray myself as an academic wonder with such words as: studious, scholarly and intellectual. This time, it was my conscience that made me decide

54

against these words. I felt they would get your hopes up too high in expecting a horn rim wearing, sliderule-toting genius destined to bring fame to the university with my academic prowess. While those adjectives are accurate to a point, they are sometimes overridden by such words as: rebellious, lazy and mischievous. I considered using these as a warning to you, but like their predecessors they seemed to over-emphasize one side of my personality while neglecting the other.

Next I decided to use a humorous approach. I tried using adjectives with radically conflicting meanings. After much thought, I settled on "brilliant", "gorgeous" and "modest." However, I could find no feasible way of explaining such a combination, so I was forced to abandon yet another idea.

Becoming somewhat frustrated, I decided to take a more liberal interpretation of the question. After all, there was nothing in the instructions that said the adjectives couldn't be made up! So I invented the words "semiomniscient" and "quasiomnipotent", but couldn't think of a third. Undaunted, I further liberalized my interpretation of the question by realizing that the words did not have to be in English, so I made up a word in German to complete my list. I came up with "ricebildperfekte" which, loosely translated, means "picture-perfect for admission to Rice."

At this point I realized that this ploy, though clever, would not quite make it. Glancing at the clock and realizing that I had been at this for several hours, I became so distraught that the only adjectives that came to mind were ones such as these: frustrated, exasperated, defeated, tired and hungry. But after a sandwich and a quick nap, I was refreshed and had a new plan. All I had to do was come up with three basic adjectives that describe me and then look them up in a thesaurus to find more glamorous sounding synonyms. Thus in no time at all "friendly, honest, and hard-working" became "amicable, veracious, and assiduous." But before I could type them up, I began to wonder: could this candy-coated version of the truth be a violation of the Rice Honor System? Not wanting to take the chance, I gave up on this idea too.

This was my darkest moment. Though I was determined to work at this until I found three adjectives, I had already come up with several different ideas, though not one of them was workable. However, I still felt that I could resolve this problem. Then suddenly I realized that all of this had in itself brought out three of my most important personality traits— perseverence, creativity, and optimism. I utilize these traits in solving any problem, including those in school. Optimism gives me enough confidence in my abilities, and perseverence and creativity work together to allow me to try all possible methods of solving the problem without giving up. In this case, confident that I could eventually come up with the three adjectives, I tried several different methods of selecting them and finally arrived at what I feel to be the most representative of myself. Thus ends my long and frustrating quest for the three elusive adjectives. Now, if I could just figure out which book or movie to write about . . .

Karen Duffy

Who (and Why) I Am

Slightly frizzy hair—usually in my face . . . foreign films
from the fourth row of the Carolina theater (where a breeze
always blows from the projector fan) . . . the lyrics of Simon
and Garfunkel's "The Sound of Silence" . . . mou no-
pycckuu . . . only eating plain hotdogs and pizza without pep-
peronis . . . pale yellow . . . my goldfish, "Aqua", who lives in a
wineglass . . . a wrinkled David Bowie poster above my
bed . . . Kurt Vonnegut books . . . James Dean in *Rebel
Without a Cause* . . . reading "The New Yorker" for its cartoons . . . music by R.E.M. . . . crying every time Ali McGraw
tells Ryan O'Neal "Love means never having to say you're
sorry" . . . $f(x)$=why? . . . jogging in the rain . . . strawberry ice
cream with M&M's . . . waking up at night, inspired to write a
line of poetry . . .passionate arguing over a physics problem . . . a.k.a. "Duff" . . . talking with my roommate until 3:00
AM about school, guys, and the meaning of life . . . bad taste
in my mouth when saying the word "conservative" . . . intense
hate of mornings and cold weather . . . what's left of John
Lennon— "You may say I'm a dreamer, but I'm not the only
one, I hope somebody you will join us . . . and the world will
live as one." . . . me.

Christa Hershman

"It doesn't matter who we say we are. You define
us in the simplest most available terms possible: a
brain, a princess, a jock, a basket case, a criminal.
But today we discovered that we are all part brain,
princess, jock, basket case, and criminal."

The Breakfast Club

The sheer number of applicants in the admissions process
forces colleges to define an applicant in the simplest, most
available terms, S.A.T. scores and grade point averages. Ultimately, however, you must choose a person, not a sum of
scores, to attend U.N.C.. In order to provide a broader scope of
information on which to base your decision, I have drawn up a
list of some of my own terms.

I. Literary Interests
   Favorite book: *Something Wicked This Way Comes* by Ray
               Bradbury
   Favorite author: John Irving
   Favorite quotation: "If we couldn't laugh we'd all go
               insane." Jimmy Buffet
   Favorite poem: "Buffalo Bill's Defunct" by e.e. cummings

II. Musical taste
   Favorite music group: past—Peter, Paul, and Mary
               present—Talking Heads
   Favorite song: The Circle Game by Joni Mitchell

III. Personal Information
   Deepest fear: Dying before I have fulfilled my potential.
   Most embarrassing moment: A salesperson mistook me for
      a young man as I searched for a strapless bra to wear
      with my prom dress.

Most valuable learning experience: team-sport competition
Worst experience: seeing my mother cry

IV. Miscellaneous
If you could be anywhere, besides typing this information, where would you be?
   Watching the sun set over the Blueridge Mountains
Most used expression: These are the vicissitudes of life.
Most preferred fashion ensemble: jeans, sweat shirt, tennies
Favorite work of art: Rodin's "The Gates of Hell"
Description of me, by a friend, in three words or less:
   "Hilariously, unequivocably, honest."

This list, as random as it may seem, defines me more clearly than any test score or academic achievement. This list defines me in the simplest, most human terms possible.

Realization Essays

How do you use your experiences to change and grow? The "realization essay" can show how thoughtful, sensitive, and responsive you are, and writing it may give you even more insight.

One incident rarely changes a person's life. Trying to persuade the reader that, for example, a single football game suddenly revolutionized your personality is likely to sound (and be) contrived rather than profound. Nevertheless, discussing a specific experience can be a great way to express a change or an idea that has developed over time.

The first essay, *Why I Love Jesus*, is an honest account of alienation. Though the tone is sometimes bitter, the cynicism is infectious. The author took a risk, to be sure, but it paid off. The admissions officer at UNC/Chapel Hill uses this essay today as an example for future writers.

Effort can be more impressive than victory. Not only do most people avoid sorting out their personal conflicts in a college essay—they don't try to sort them out in real life. In the second essay, someone is really trying, and that makes her impressive.

Jesse Matz wrote an essay that struck home to the greatest number of our preliminary readers. It has excellent insight, but its strongest attribute is Jesse's ability to dissolve bitterness with humor and understanding.

Jennifer Dodge, in her "Whomp!" essay, turns a broken leg and a potentially ruined year into an enlightening experience. She avoids syrupy glorifications of her admirable deed and maintains an upbeat, cheerful tone through the difficult topics of pain and charity.

The essay on procrastination struck home with us (just ask our publisher). We identified with the writer while laughing with him, and the self-recognition made the humor even richer. The admissions officer told us, "I chuckled with delight upon reading this essay, was swept away by the language, and jumped up from my chair and rushed into the hallway to share it with my colleagues."

Shubla Shukla's *Polygon Effect* deals with a common problem in our nation's bi-cultural homes. In a light-hearted look at growing up as an Indian-American, she gives an interesting glimpse into a world we might never have seen. And Claire Riccardi uses her journeys to strange places to emphasize the stability of her ideals. Her beautiful essay is profound and revealing.

Melanie Sumner

Why I Love Jesus

Around the age of 13, I was transformed from a little sun-shine into something equivalent to Satan's spawn. I do not know why I suddenly began saying, "shut-up", smoking cigarettes, and attending Sunday School alone in the church parking lot. My mother was convinced that it was the hand of Lucifer. Something had to be done.

Our church, a down-home, folksy, Baptist one, was having a Youth Retreat. A Youth Retreat is a weekend spent somewhere in the boonies where youths can have fun and rededicate their lives to God. Fledglings to the house of God and old-timers that have strayed from the path are particularly encouraged to come. I was one of the strays. My mother saddled me with pencils, several variations of the Bible, a helpful little book en-titled *Why I Love Jesus*, and, at the last minute, a frisbee. I was then packed off with a dozen other youths to Gatlinburg, Tennessee.

The bus ride to Gatlinburg was not too bad. I pretended that I loved Jesus too and enjoyed spitting spitballs, climbing upon the luggage racks, and screaming, "McDonald's!" with the rest of the youths. My "McDonald's" did not sound like theirs, though. They all pronounced the "a" with a drawn out twang. Eventually, as it is usually does with this age group, the conversation turned to school. The twang got louder, and I heard someone say "ain't". "Where ya going to school?" I was awakened from my intense study of a nearby girl's Dock-siders. The stiching was different; they were not real Docksid-ers at all. I decided that the shoes were a forgery, an economy brand from K-Mart. I had delayed in answering the casual question, and now all eyes were upon me.

"Uh, Darlington*," I mumbled. There was a slight silence. It was an ugly word. Darlington meant money, preppy clothes, and smart people: Heathens mostly. Since I was a snob from Darlington, most of the young disciples didn't speak to me for the rest of the weekend.

The lodge for our Youth Retreat was situated on top of a grassy hillside, complete with mountainous views and clean, swirling streams that ended in tranquil blue pools. I was impressed. If there were a God, I certainly might find Him in these celestial surroundings. The church leaders had other things in mind. As always, there was a smattering of wholesome religious fun. Fun was mandatory. Several times during the day we were all compelled to gather around a tarnished, tuneless piano and sing to Jesus. Young faces glowing with the love of Christ turned to glare at me because I was not singing. I personally thought Jesus would have better taste in music.

We also played a softball game. This game was organized with hidden Christian motives by Lennie The Youth Director. Lennie was short, pink, pudgy Christian who giggled, "O.K. gang, are we ready for Bible softball?"

"Ain't never heard of it," replied a wayward youngster. Evidently Lennie saw humor in this because he had a mild fit of giggling. Then with unrestrained joy at having invented such a novel game, he exclaimed, "You guys are gonna be Philistines and Israelites!" He emitted another silly giggle. I began to doubt the authenticity of his gender. Is God like that? What if God is a nerd? We played Bible softball, and I was exiled the second inning for uttering pagan words after my third strike. I was marched back to the lodge by a Youth Director Assistant and ordered to repent and wait for Lennie.

I decided to repent while exploring the surrounding forest of our camp. It was calm in the woods, and I enjoyed wandering around and climbing upon the huge rock formations scattered about. I settled myself on a particularly comfortable rock and decided to try and find God. I considered my numerous sins and transgressions, and failing to find any way to redeem

---

*Darlington is an elite preparatory school in a small town in northwest Georgia.

myself, I began searching through my pockets for a Winston Light. A few puffs of a cigarette always seemed to clear my mind.

Lennie was not his smiling self when I found my way back to our group of cabins. Everyone had gone to the streets of Gatlinburg to convert bad people by singing to them and giving away free "God Loves You" mugs. Lennie thought we should have a little talk or "rap" as he put it. I thought not and so tried to speed things up by congenially admitting to being the Antichrist. Lennie The Youth Director was not amused. I endeavored to make him feel more comfortable by gigglng. I do not think he liked me much after that.

The last night of every Youth Retreat is the biggest. It is an evening of burning confession and mass conversion. The night was hot and coal black as we all seated ourselves around the huge bonfire. Lennie gave an inspiring sermon warning us that time is short. The amber red of the roaring flames reflected on the circle of little Christian faces. It reminded me of hell. At last the preaching drew to a close and the finale was upon us.

"If you feel that Gawd has touched your heart, come; come and promise your soul to Him. He is calling one and all. Yes, He is calling you!" There was some nervous whispering and murmurs of "Reckon we gotta . . . " The first little lamb edged her way forward and the rest followed noisily, like a herd of dirty, stupid sheep. They all went. They were all called, all touched by the mysterious hand of the Lord. Each renewed believer walked to the center of the ever narrowing circle to shake Lennie's hand and sit closer to the fire—closer so that if you squinted your eyes it looked like they were in the fire, holding Lennie's hand, smiling. The fire burned lower until there was only a flicker among the charred embers. And still one black soul sat away from the saved ones, one black one still believed.

(Name Withheld)

Sometimes I think about all the things that have
happened to me in my life and I wonder . . . what would the
kids at school think if they knew that (Name)—straight
A+(Name) the Brain whohastopgradesandherparentsnever-
bughersowhatmorecouldshewant—spent most of her childhood
crying and feeling inferior because no one ever wanted to play
with her or go to the mall or do normal kid things or be her
friend and that the reason those grades were so important was
that they were all she had? What would people say if they
knew that my mom got divorced because she was a manic
depressive and had to be hospitalized leaving little me and my
baby sister in the care of Nana, who never liked Mommy and
said mean things and made me cry into my pillow at night?

I remember when after living with her parents and getting
better, Mom brought us home to be with her. I loved my
special family. My grandparents weren't just faceless people in
Florida who sent me presents every year. I thought things
were perfect. I was very young then. In time I realized that
Grandma and Grandpa were running the show, and although I
loved them there were many things I didn't like about them:
they were narrow-minded, hermitish, and they didn't trust
Mom. I did, until she got sick in 1980. I felt scared and hurt
by some of the things she said and did, and even after she got
better it was a long time before I trusted her again. The whole
situation began to improve when Mom started to date and to
work part-time. I even hoped that we would be able to move
out someday and be like a normal single-parent family.

(When I was sixteen, my dad, who was only forty-two but
had high blood pressure and never went to the doctor no matter how much I cried, had a fatal stroke. Just when I was old
enough to talk to him and get to know him as a person, I was
cheated out of it, and I was mad as hell at him. I didn't even
get to say goodbye.)

Nothing really changed, though. It was still Grandpa's house, and he was still in charge. I was angry at Mom for not standing up to him. Two years ago, Grandma got lung cancer. At first they didn't even tell me what it was. I don't know why I kept thinking she was getting better; I guess I didn't want to believe that Grandma would be gone so soon after Daddy. It wasn't until three months after the doctors gave up hope that Mom shouted at me "Don't you realize she's going to die?" and I did. The other unfair part was that Mom was finally ready to leave, and we couldn't. She said it would be different afterward. Grandpa would mellow and let her have more control. That was something I counted on when I was so stifled in the house that I could barely breathe, when my head pounded constantly and I ran out almost every night just to find some space to *be*.

Grandma died a few weeks ago, and for a couple of days sadness was eased by relief. Then Mom started to get sick, and our plans followed Grandpa's trust in her right out the window. I understand the immediate cause this time, so it doesn't hurt as much, but I still get angry and yell at her a lot. I guess I'm just feeling cheated, again.

I've written these things down for the first ever, and cried as I remembered some of them, and it seems hard to believe I've only been alive for seventeen years. Sometimes I get so sick of things happening to me that I want to scream (and many times I do). That's one reason I'm so anxious to get to college. I can't change my childhood into the one I wanted but next year I will be out on my own and I will finally have the chance to make my life turn out the way I plan it.

Jesse Matz

Ever watch "My Three Sons" on T.V.? I'm not an avid television viewer, but whenever I'd watch it when I was little it always struck me as rather odd. "Pop" always smiled benevolently and gave wise counsel over dinner, while meals with my own "Pop" always consisted of an awkward silence occasionally punctuated by a sarcastic remark from my father in some impersonal restaurant. Just recently, however, my father and I met for dinner after a long and regrettable estrangement; what happened that night played more like a scene from "My Three Sons" than anything of my previous experience, and my reactions to it made me understand both my father and myself with greater insight and maturity than ever before.

Perhaps all children see their parents as demi-gods capable of incredible feats but incapable of fault or weakness. I'd always seen my father that way, but was awakened from this somewhat euphoric state early in my childhood when my parents' divorce and my father's apparent neglect shattered my ideal of fatherly perfection. Not only did my father not measure up to Fred MacMurray, but he seemed to have nothing but faults. My attitude spilled over into other areas of my young life; just as Plato had conceived of a perfect example of everything in his Theory of Forms, a little Jesse had already established in his minds certain idealistic standards for all people and things in his life. I must admit, these standards of perfection made me a somewhat compulsive little boy who was often left disillusioned.

The differences between my father and myself were further aggravated by a conflict of interests: Dad would visit on weekends, dragging me away from a good book for a game of baseball where my ineptitude left me feeling deeply embarrassed. In a way, though, I believe what I saw as my father's un-intellectuality made me strive all the more in the opposite direction. "Chip" may have had a sweet and doting father, but I'm willing to bet my socks that "Chip" can't read ancient Greek!

Thus, I found myself a bit surprised and confused when my father and I finally began to communicate. He told me that, although we didn't have common interests, he held a greater regard for mine, that he admired and was almost jealous of my strength of will in resisting his influence and in pursuing what I loved. He apologized for his inability to communicate and for the neglect that had prevented a close relationship between us, and he told me that he'd always been proud of me, of my achievements and performances and of the person I had become.

As he spoke, I realized that the very fact that we were speaking meant that I, too, had long since purged the choler of my disillusioned resentment that had maintained the wall between us. This reconciliation left me feeling good, not only about my father but about myself. I understood how I had changed from a cynical little tot into an optimistic young man. I realize now that hoping for perfection, that creating idols, is a frustrating and fruitless pursuit; I am even grateful for imperfections in the people and things that I love because those imperfections allow me to more fully understand what love is, and because I sense that my own imperfections, too, are forgivable. This fall, I was outraged by a change my school had implemented in the direction of a more standardized cur- riculum, a change decidedly for the worse. I channeled my energy into a constructive campaign to rally student support and to offer alternate solutions. I was able to do this because I had come to realize that an institution may be flawed but still amenable to change, and that it is everyone's responsibili- ty to work to perfect it rather than wallow in disillusioned resignation.

Perhaps my early experience of having my ideals shattered helped me to develop a realistic outlook. After a period of disillusionment, I believe I matured into a heightened awareness of myself and others. Compassion and self- awareness are qualities I prize most and ones that in some measure I now possess.

Whereas I was once an exacting perfectionist, I have grown into a person with an almost pathological need to understand and help other people. It is almost as if I am making up for lost time which I spent expecting too much from others; my adolescent life been spent in efforts, both on a personal level and in schoolwide activities, to make others feel comfortable with themselves and proud of their own achievements. I believe very strongly in modesty and social courtesy; at the very least boasting makes others uncomfortable. My tendency to strive for excellence, however, has not disappeared, but evolved: now I see being "perfect" as being tolerant and compassionate, towards others and towards myself.

I believe that all children deify their parents and that part of growing up involves the gradual acceptance of faults. It may be that my parents' divorce interrupted this natural flow in my own life, but it also hastened it. I am better off having grown up with obstacles, and my reconciliation with my father has provided a vantage point from which I can look back and understand that I have finally achieved a balance between acceptance and perfectionism. Looking back now, I can't believe that I ever compared such a decent and complex man as my father to some two-dimensional character on a T.V. program that never got particularly good ratings anyway. And, when you get right dowm to it, how great could a man be if he names his son "Chip?"

Jennifer Dodge

It is tempting to describe myself to you in terms of grades, more lists of extracurricular activities, to expound on my love of reading, to, in fact, try to wow you with my attributes. But I'm uncomfortable with that, and you still wouldn't know any more about me as a person. I'm going to try to give you some insight into me by relating one experience and its ramifications.

My friends and I have a special word to perfectly describe an "ah hah experience". The word is Whomp! (You pronounce the wh as if you are saying what.) We use this word to describe what happens when something really hits you hard. For example: "I left my Accounting project at home, and home, and, Whomp!, Mrs. Winslow gave me *six* extra assignments as a consequence!" Or, "I couldn't believe he took her out. Whomp! It's really over between us."

Okay. I hope you now have an idea of the significance of the word. With that as background I can tell you about the biggest Whomp! of my life. It happened early in October, 1984, during my junior year. I was with a group of friends at a cabin in the hills of Eastern Iowa. While standing on a balcony approximately thirty-five feet above the rocky terrain, the supports under the balcony gave way. Luckily for me, the ground broke my fall; unluckily, my leg did the same. One minute I was a healthy, mobile sixteen year old and, Whomp!, the next I had a leg in about fourteen different pieces, with some of those pieces protruding through a gaping wound.

My memories of the next few days are rather hazy. I can remember my mother's worried face hovering over me from time to time. I remember being told that I'd been through surgery and that they'd (the wondrous orthopedists) packed the bones together and fastened them at each end with pins. "Cool. You'll beep the airport metal detectors, Jen," my brother told me. Well, I'd also have sore armpits (crutches became my best friend and worst brother), and a cast up to my hip for six months. It seemed like an eternity.

Physical pain was the least of my worries. Whomp! People stared at me now. I couldn't take a shower. I couldn't go jogging. I couldn't stand for very long. I couldn't be on the track team. I couldn't get down to the newspaper room at school. I could watch TV—small compensation. I felt totally helpless and very frustrated at times. I needed help getting dressed, and getting to class, and getting into the car . . .

Wait a minute, this cast is only going to be on for six more months. Whomp! Some people are like this for their entire life. Some people have much worse problems that they must deal with every day of their existence with no light at the end of a six-month tunnel.

This really got me thinking. What would it be like to be physically handicapped? Dependent your whole life? These insights made me want to get involved. They made me want to do something to make a difference.

Now it's my senior year. Handicapped students (trainably mentally retarded kids, some with physical handicaps too) have been brought to Westside for their Special Education classes. I went to see the Department Head of Special Education. Together we devised a club called Peer Advocates which is like a buddy system between the regular education and special education kids. We have tried to pair the non-handicapped with the handicapped students according to interests and personalities. They are required to spend at least four hours a month with their match. We are also planning several group field trips to places like the zoo and bowling.

Organizing this group has been one of the most meaningful things I've ever done. Now kids of two totally different lifestyles are going out to lunch together and learning things about each other that they could never have learned from reading a book or studying handicaps. We are all learning compassion and tolerance and understanding. As for myself, I feel as though I'm doing something extremely worthwhile. For example, one morning, after a breakfast meeting of the group, a boy with Downs Syndrome named David walked up to me with a huge smile and gave me a great bear hug. He told me that he was so happy to have a special friend at Westside and thanked me. That was all I needed to know that the idea had been a good one.

Breaking my leg and its aftermath of pain and frustration was one experience I'd never want to go through again. But what it taught me was invaluable and I wouldn't change it for the world. It was a definite Whomp!

Christopher Harwood

There is a little demon that lurks in my conscious and unconscious mind that has done me more ill than any conventional ailment could. It is a stealthy creature that preys upon weakness and appetite and has ruined many a fair weekend in my life, and in the lives of many. The demon's name is procrastination, and he mocks me even as I type up the final draft of this essay. For the demon has triumphed again, and stolen my sleep, and he may triumph again after this. But I think not for a while, for this time he has stung me sorely, and my guard shall be up.

This autumn and winter have been a hectic time in my life, and the hectic time is when the demon thrives. In late October I began rehearsal for a play. The rehearsal schedule was not rigorous at first, and did not rule my life, but it was there. It was there and the demon seized upon it and assured me I had nothing to worry about; January and deadline time was still a long way off. And I was persuaded, and the further into rehearsal I went, the less I resisted the imp's devious advice. It was not long into reheasal when the other, smaller deadlines began to creep up and rear their ugly heads, and paper after paper after test struck me unmercifully. And then the play was over. It was almost Christmas and now the responsibilities of shopping allied themselves with my academic obligations and thrashed me mercilessly while the demon chuckled, knowing that the real dealine was obscured and would be staggeringly painful to meet. Finally. Christmas was past, and the real deadline loomed ahead, frighteningly unobscured. Now the diabolical creature convulsed in unrestrained laughter, while I shuddered with a tinge of fear of imminent discomfort.

I then began the ordeal that would geometrically increase my misery daily until the Epiphany, when the deadline must be met. I cursed the demon, loudly at first, then more softly and then not at all. I stopped and I could only laugh an ironic laugh. For I realized that the demon does not exist; that he is merely an apparition that I have created. And discovering the power of creation I realized that I also have the power to dispell the creature. I know now that all I need do is seize the deadline in the distance and never shall the demon haunt me.

Shubla Shulka

The Polygon Effect

"Where are you from?"

For the average Joe, this question requires little critical thought—he automatically finds his mouth forming the words Pottawattamie, Iowa, Barcelona, Spain, or Ulaanbaatar, Mongolia.

For me, however, this simple question requires much thought and usually causes me great conflict. Should I say, "I'm from the United States," or should I say, "I'm from India"? Maybe I should be more specific and answer, "I was born and raised in the United States, but my parents are from India."

Well, I knew from the start, when I was a wee lass still experimenting with the joys of finger-painting, that life, or rather my life, was full of contradictions. You see, this tiny tot had the fortune of being born into an Indian family living in the United States.

This means more than munching on chutney sandwiches while intently watching the "Brady Bunch," or listening to my Walkman clad in paisley, or burning incense while scouring the depths of Steinbeck. Balancing conflicting ideas and beliefs while conforming to the demands of both cultures has made me the unique person that I am.

When visiting India, I always find that there's far more to culture shock than dealing with the cows in the airport. Although my relatives refer to me as their "American relative," I am, by all means, expected to behave like their Indian relative. So, when I trip down the stairs in a sari, I'm greeted with hysterical laughter instead of a comforting smile. And even though I've spent months at home in the U.S. practicing my Hindi until it's fluent and flawless, when I get to our home town in India, I am faced with a barrage of questions spoken in a dialect that could be Greek for all I know.

Here in America my problems are similar. One of the worst things has been having to answer cliched questions all my life. When I was younger it was usually, "Did you live in a mud hut in India?" Now, however, I get more advanced questions like, "Why do Indian women have a dot on their foreheads?" Some of my friends even think that being a different religion means getting twice the number of holidays! But, the biggest problem comes with doing the everyday things that young American people do. When I go to a football game or a school dance, even though my parents will smile and say, "Have a good time," I know that they are wondering if I am slowly losing my Indian culture. How do I explain to them that I am not losing my Indian heritage—that I'm just gaining another culture?

But I waved away that persistant fly called self-pity long ago. I have more than India and the United States; I have the whole planet if I want it. So, in order to find myself, I lose myself in the world, and now my landscape of knowledge consists of soil collected from a myriad of cultures. Life is a polygon, and if I can see and understand it from two different sides, I can see and understand it from any side.

Since birth I have been immune to ethnocentricity, a dreaded disease that afflicts many a soul and often leads to misunderstanding between different cultures. Once, I came across an advanced case of the aforementioned disease while browsing in a tourist shop in Germany. A large, gaudily dressed man, the epitome of a typical American tourist, came marching into the shop waving a map, and demanded that someone tell him what the hell was written on that map and why it was that Germans couldn't do anything right. He proceeded to harrass the poor man at the counter, and upon discovering that he couldn't speak English, he shook his head and said, "These stupid Germans can't even speak English!" He then stomped out of the shop. Another similar incident occurred at Heathrow Airport in London. While waiting at the baggage claims department, I noticed a small group of Indians squeezing their way into the front of the line. With the overpopulation in India, most people don't have time to wait in lines and will do anything to get ahead. But what is acceptable in one country isn't necessarily acceptable in another, and this is what they didn't realize.

At first I felt shame for both the American man and the group of Indians and was embarrassed that they were representatives of my nations. The shame soon turned to sympathy, however, as I realized that their actions were probably the result of an inexposure to different cultures.

So, little old bicultural me has learned to take advantage of my curious combination of cultures. Rather than lose myself in the vast chasm that divides my worlds, this kid has managed to plant a firm foot on each side, and stand tall about it all. I am now ready to face almost any challenge that comes my way.

Claire Riccardi

A risk is a suspension; a flight; a going-somewhere. You can either forget how to fly or you can learn how. A risk is learning.

Landing in the New Delhi airport was less than romantic. The flight, usually two days long, was delayed in Frankfurt; consequently I was not exactly awake on arrival. The plane taxied to a stop on the runway, not next to the terminal, so we had to get off onto makeshift stairs put up against the side of the plane. The night was hot and wet, and I remember how the handrails and the ground sweated with the damp so that I half-walked, half-slid down the steps.

It wasn't an airport. It was several large, yellowish crumbling rooms punctuated with thick ugly pillars, around which crouched skinny young boys playing marbles and sprawling families waiting to get through customs. Because my father was in the diplomatic service, all I saw before we were whisked through was a boy stalking a huge cockroach with a stick. My father showed his passport, the child raised his weapon, and we were out the door and gone into the sweaty night.

During the rainy season, India is wet and fertile. After months of clogging dry dust and cracked brown earth the sudden explosion of lush green is incredible and frightening to see. In a country where life is fragile and deprivation is a way of existence for thousands the steaming grasses and clinging foliage are somehow obscene, and yet they do represent the country's amazing ability to replenish its life. For me, it was completely alien.

Arriving in the Port Authority bus terminal was also less than romantic. Even though I knew that I would be living with my father, it had been raining; I was scared and wet and lonely and I felt incompetent, which didn't help. New York City is frightening, I don't care what anybody says; for the newcomer it's huge and bald and very hostile. The subways are clanging metal boxes packed full of apparently genetically miserable people who, heads exploding with noise and tedium, sway back and forth against each others' shrinking bodies. This wasn't just alien, it scared me.

I've always had certain values—love, honesty, trust—that I never questioned. I didn't need to; they were woven into my environment and had never been challenged. Moving physically from home made me examine them; forced me to decide what was really important to me. In India and in New York I discovered that the state of mind that I had previously called normal had disappeared and I was starting all over in organizing my priorities. It was a little like being a bottle of salad dressing—sitting for awhile, thinking I'd finally got it all together, when in reality everything of value had sunk to the bottom of the jar. Being uprooted stirred me up and made me realize that my values weren't dependent on an environment, that I could go anywhere and they'd still be apart of me. That gave me a trust and a confidence in myself that I hadn't had before.

Off-Beat Essays

These essays are bizzare. From flies to Oreos to mismatched socks, the essays in this section use off-the-wall material to enliven the application and showcase the student's wit.

The playful mood and memorable images of David Bolognia's *Nightly Ritual* and David Gordon's *Socks* are wonderful. Without getting repetitive, they explore all the possibilities of their topics, and they are wise enough to end the essay before the reader stops laughing. Both were picked as the year's best by their respective colleges, Rice and Johns Hopkins.

Matt Weingarten's *One Act Musical* had one of the most original formats we have seen. It is a clever, confident applicant who can submit an essay like this because, as a Yale English professor remarked, "Not many application writers have the nerve to rhyme 'accept' with 'adept,' or admit they have a friend named 'Sponge.' "

The *Move your ass!* essay is another very risky piece, but it works well. One admissions officer said, "I can't remember an essay in the past few months that has gotten so many genuine laughs of commiseration and relief. There is something about this essay that stops you dead in your tracks and makes you kick back for a minute and think about the entire process." We should note that the author wrote a longer, more serious piece for the second essay on his application.

Joe Clifford's *Metaphor for Life* is just plain funny and may show the value of reading Woody Allen before sitting down to write. Although Joe's philosophy may not appeal to everyone, his analysis of the article "the" stands above dispute. In the next piece, Gregg Shapiro, by introducing a unique pet, employed a comical, unusual image to make his essay memorable.

Each essay in this section replies in a quirky, maybe even flippant, tone to the question. The writer's wit becomes his selling point. But the off-beat essay can easily backfire. Dan Lundquist, an admissions officer at the University of Pennsylvania, warns that many "witty" essays are not funny, and admissions officers view them as inappropriate or even obnoxious.

Submitting an off-beat essay is a big gamble, but it can reward handsomely if it's good. Our advice: let a lot of people read your essay before you send it, and make sure everyone else thinks it's as hilarious and ingenious as you do.

David Bolognia

My Nightly Ritual
(Heretofore Kept Secret)

The best thing to eat day or night, winter or summer, anywhere in the world, at anytime, inside, outside, or upside
down, alone, or with a friend, is an Oreo cookie. I do not refer
to any Oreo cookie, but to the singularly succulent sustenance
which retains its number one position on the weekly top-forty
goody list, month after month. Of course, I refer to the extremely palatable Doublestuff. Being a self-taught connoisseur
of this craft, I will share my experiences on exactly how to eat
these desirous, delectable delights.

First and foremost, I make extra sure Mom has them on her
shopping list weekly. Oreos without milk is like Laurel without Hardy, so obviously, the second requirement is milk; it
must be cold and it must be fresh. The glass in which to pour
the milk must be short and fat, not tall and thin, for dunking
purposes, of course. If the preliminary steps have been com-
pleted and my perspicacious dog has not discovered my inten-
tions yet, it only means more for me. (There are ways to trick
even the wisest of dogs, but let us not digress here.)

Once all the materials are gathered, I recline in a dimly lit
room and pig out. Taking one at a time so as to relish every
bite makes for a most memorable event. I never eat the whole
cookie right away because much can be told about a person by
the way he eats his Doublestuffs, and this method designates
a boring personality.

First, I turn the chocolate cookie part in a clockwise direction and pull lightly, never pulling too hard so as to break it. I
dunk half the chocolate piece in the milk, eat it, and toss the
remaining half to appease the dog drooling on my leg. At this
point, depending on the mood and company, there are different

methods to follow. If time is short, I dunk the rest of the cookie, quickly swirling it so as to soften it and plop the whole piece in my mouth. If I feel its weakening, the process is even quicker, because there is nothing worse than slugged milk. It is imperative to remember that a cookie in the mouth is worth two in the glass.

The classic style in Nabisco is the "bucky-beaver bite." It is done by scraping the front teeth down across the white cream paying particular attention to what is done so as not to bump the nose on the hard cookie. Once it is on my tongue, I fling my head back, swallowing it delicately. Of course, this method leaves another plain chocolate cookie, which the dog will gladly devour.

However, my all time favorite method of eating an Oreo is to build a bigger cookie; we have the technology. For this more complicated process, a butterknife is a necessity. The disassembling process is repeated. Now both chocolate sections must be removed from subsequent cookies. Here the butterknife comes in handy. This must be done gently so as not to break the cookie. The cream fillings are to be carefully stacked one on top of the other until guilt sets in or it no longer fits in the mouth. There is an option of eating the extra chocolates or gaining a life long friend in the now salivating dog. After admiring my creation, I "dunk-n-devour."

Lastly, every drop of milk is consumed while searching for drowning bits and pieces. Now I rinse the glass and take a follow-up swig of clean, fresh milk.

Following these easy instructions, even the most simple-minded person can become a creditable cookie consumer. Using any of these methods, I encourage everyone to partake in this epicurean delight. I am positive if all the men, women, and children of this world were to join in the sublime ritual of this art, we would have the happiest planet in the Milky Way. And now I feel this overwhelming urge to retire to the kitchen for more research.

David Gordon

Socks

If I had the power to eliminate one problem in this world it would be getting rid of the sock takers in washing machines. I don't know what it is, but every time I get my laundry back, no matter what I do, there's always at least one sock without its mate. It's so frustrating.

Often I will sort the other laundry first and hold the socks until the end. That way I can make sure no socks are stuck to anything else, eliminating a lot of unnecessary anxiety and false alarms. When I do get a single sock my first inclination is to find the other one. I get very anxious that I might not find its mate. Sometimes, it'll just be stuck to my shirt or wrapped around the crotch of my underwear, giving me a strong sense of relief.

If I can't complete the pair I get a very empty feeling almost as if I were abandoned. Then I have a problem. I can't throw it out because if I do, the other one will undoubtedly turn up.

A little while ago as we were packing to move to a new house I contemplated throwing out a couple of singles that were sitting in my drawer. I figured that the chaos of the move would surely eliminate any chances of finding the mates for these knitted bachelors. So I threw them out. After we settled in our new house, just as if the Farmer's Almanac predicted it, the other halves turned up.

The sock conundrum all starts in grade school when—if your parents haven't already scolded you for wearing mismatched socks—one of your classmates will, in front of the entire school. After weathering that for a day, you secretly vow never to do that again.

Then you spend your life being sure that your socks always match. There are only a few times you can wear mismatched socks. You do it for a reason, telling everyone and being very self-conscious. The only time I ever wore mismatched socks was when I wanted to "psych out" my opponents in a soccer game. It really bothered them, too.

One time I tried to outsmart the sock takers by buying all white tube socks with no stripes and no heels. I figured I'd show them. For a while I had the problem licked. But after I used them a few times, each pair began to look a little different. One pair was a little brown from wearing it with my Docksides. Another was grey from the dirt of a soccer game. And one was light blue on the bottom from wearing it in the rain with my sneakers.

As soon as each pair had its own identity the sock takers struck again. When I tried interchanging them, I discovered each sock had married itself to another and just didn't look right with any other relative.

My younger brother has the sock problem too. He keeps his singles in a little stack with a rubber band around them, and he hasn't thrown one out yet. Dad's are in a special section, segregated from the pairs, in the front left corner of his drawer. Even Mom, who really doesn't have many socks, has her little accumulation in a special place in her bureau.

No one can admit they have a sock problem. Even in a place like the laundrymat where people air the most scandalous gossip, you will never find them admitting that they can't keep track of their socks.

Can you imagine what would happen if everyone started talking about it? Whole new fields of psychiatry would open up. Followers of Freud would now practice socko-analysis.

Madison Avenue would come out with a whole slew of products to combat the problem. They would come up with all sorts of ingenious remedies. Pampers would probably hit the streets first with new disposable socks. Then would come all the fastening versions in snap, lace, velcro or button styles. It wouldn't be long before Maytag would come out with an ultra-modern deluxe laundry machine specially equipped with a locking sock cage. You'll know that things have gotten completely out of hand when your car admonishes politely and unsympathetically: "Your socks are mismatched . . . "

Matt Weingarden
_____

An Untitled One-Act Musical

characters:
Matt, a Yale applicant
Sponge, his closest friend
a Chorus of their fellow high-school students
Scene: a Cranbook School corridor. Matt and Sponge sit
against a wall; students walk by in both directions.

Matt: I've decided that I want to go to Yale. It's got
everything I want—a good Classics department, a
good English department, great science facilities—
and from what I hear, it offers the best
undergraduate education in the country. I'm not sure
exactly what I'll major in—probably Classics or
Classics and English—but it's important to me that
the college I attend be strong in every area, because
of my wide range of interests. I'll take a variety of
courses: math, science, English, Latin, Greek, art,
music. I want the best, most challenging education
to be had, and I think I'll find it in New Haven.
Sponge: Fantastic. I hope you get in.
Chorus: (stopping abruptly in the hallway and singing to the
tune of "When Johnny Comes Marching Home")
Oh, Matt is applying to Yale on his knees,
Accept! Accept!
Academically, socially, artistically, he's
Adept! Adept!
With his sharp sense of humor he knocks us all out,
He is a candidate we highly tout
And our song may be stale
But Matt ought to get into Yale. (students com-
mence walking again)

Matt: Yeah, I hope I get in, too. I'm a little worried about it.

Sponge: Oh, I don't think you have anything to worry about. I mean, you're one of the best students in the school, you're involved in all those extracurriculars, you play guitar, you write, you draw and paint, you're an accomplished intramural athlete—what more could they want?

Chorus: (stopping again and singing to the tune of "My Bonnie Lies Over the Ocean")
While Matt prays for his Yale acceptance,
The Sponge thinks he's wasting his time,
Old Sponge says there will be no problem,
But Matt feels he need be sublime.
Take him, Take him,
We hope you decide to admit our Matt,
Take him, Take him,
We hope you accept our friend Matt. (they continue walking)

Matt: Don't be naive, Sponge. There are so many applicants that are more qualified than I am and the decisions are based on so many criteria—I just don't know. (stands) C'mon. We'll be late for Physics. (begins singing softly to the tune of "My Favorite Things")
Baseball and Latin, Frank Zappa and eating,
Science and drawing and writing and reading,
While playing at poker to be dealt four kings,
These are a few of my favorite things . . .
(Exeunt.)

Barry Kaye

(Question: What is the best piece of advice you've ever received?)

"Move your ass!" yelled a man as a car was bearing down on a five year old boy who was about to cross the street. That boy was me, and, needless to say, I took his advice and moved. As far as I'm concerned, that was the best piece of advice I've ever been given, for had I not received it, I would not be here today to say so.

The second best piece of advice I ever received was from my uncle, who said, "Barry, go to Medical School."

If I am not accepted to the University of Pennsylvania solely on the basis of this truthful answer, so be it. If I had not taken the man's advice, I would have gotten to Medical School anyway. As a cadaver.

Joe Clifford

Metaphor for Life

Being so naive as to not have already developed a handy
metaphorical philosophy on life, I consider myself fortunate to
have stumbled upon one while watching television this
weekend. Our television is located in a "sun room" —a room
dominated by window space. Anyway, I heard a fly buzzing. It
must have been a healthy fly because it was January 4. The
point is, extraordinary health not withstanding, this was your
typical, stupid fly. That's because the fly proceeded to get
himself stuck in between a window and the venetian blind
covering the window. Ninety-nine percent of flies who enter
our "sun room" manage to place themselves in this com-
promising position. It's actually quite sad. I can really sym-
pathize with such a fly's plight.

Anyway, after I killed this particular winter fly with a
rolled-up newspaper, I started thinking and this led to great
dividends—unerringly the result of any meditation that
originates due to observation of the insect world, a world that
is vastly underestimated by the general public. But I don't
scoff at the worth of insects and for this reason I decided to
base my philosophy on flies. Here it is: "We are, all of us, flies
trapped between the venetian blind and the window."

I suppose magnification of the ramifications of my
philosophy are in order. I think the best way to dissect my
philosopy shall be to examine it, word by word.

First "We." This means every human being on Earth, no ex-
ceptions whatsoever.

"Are." The more observant will notice that this is a verb. The
truly elite will recognize this as a verb which links the aforementioned pronoun to future modifiers.

",All of us," The commas here should clue you in. This is a handy grammatical trick that I used to emphasize the recently discussed universal scope of my deceivingly simple pronoun "We."

"Flies." Obviously, a key word. By saying "flies" I am transferring all the physical, mental and spiritual qualities of flydom onto humanity. This is a literary debt which I owe to Kafka with "Metaphorsis," Ionesco with "Rhinoceros" and Kurt Neumann, the director of the wondrous 1958 existential sci-fi movie "The Fly."

"Trapped." Another key word. It may refer to a claustrophobic helplessness in the human condition. It may refer to an absurd, no-way-out, Sisyphian nightmare or reality. It may also refer to Mel Tillis.

"Between." Relates closely to "trapped" and also "venetian blind" and "window." Seems to suggest that flies (AKA humanity) are in a hard place, so to speak. To cite a classical allusion—between Scylla and Charybdis.

"The." only an article. Nothing to get uptight about.

"Venetian blind." Caution. Heavy symbolism enters at this point. What a venetian blind is to a fly, so are clocks and watches to humans. Palpable time is a horrendous thing, something that erodes man to a powerless, devitalized shell.

"And." A conjunction.

"The." Once more, an article.

"Window." Again, be warned—deep symbolic commentary ahead. What a window is to a fly, so is realization of morality to a man. Already trapped on one side by clocks, man, like a fly, looks at the other alternative. The fly says "Oh no. There's a window. I'm doomed." Man says, "Oh no, There's my mortality. I better be extra careful." He sets restrictions and limits. He is trapped.

There you have my metaphorical philosophy. You may agree with me or you may think I'm a jerk. But ask yourself one question— "What time is it?"

Gregg Shapiro

I'm glad you gave this opportunity to express a personal concern. Since I'm going off to college next year, my mom says that I've got to get rid of my pet elephant. She's tired of him tracking mud into the house, and he's getting too big for the bathtub. Also, now that he's been fired from the car wash, he's not bringing in any money. But Renaldo and I have become quite attached, so I was wondering if it's possible for him to attend Rice. He's quite bright, and he'll get along well with the other students.

Maybe you can offer him an athletic scholarship. I'm sure the football team could use an extra extra wide receiver. Once Renaldo gets the ball he's not easy to tackle. Besides, when he's not playing, he'll make a great bench warmer.

Even a work-study program is agreeable to him. He's great at hosing down sidewalks and pulling weeds, and Ren's willing to work for peanuts. Not only that, but Renaldo's a "well-rounded" student too, head and trunk above the rest. He's got an incredible memory stored in those floppy ears.

On the undergraduate level he'd like to study public speaking, the romance languages, water resources management, gas dynamics, and sculpting. He also wants to learn typing and knitting. Ballet just isn't for him anymore.

Outside of the classroom he enjoys playing water polo. The last time he ran track a few people got shaken up so they made him quit. He still enjoys jogging around the house though. It keeps his weight down. By the way, how much would the meal plan cost?

Eventually, after graduation, Renaldo hopes to attend medical school, where he will study pachydermatology.

As you can see Renaldo's got a nice student profile. He's intelligent, active, and unique. And if he doesn't keep up with the work, we can always use him as a shower.

Thought Essays

The serious, philosophical "thought essay" is perhaps the most difficult to write. The best examples demonstrate an intellectually curious and disciplined mind, but even the best can be hard to read. Frequently, the work loses its impact because students digress from the original point and allow their logic to become muddled by "$10 words" and complicated strings of sentences.

Most students get too abstract when they discuss philosophical concepts. When you write about abstract ideas, link the idea to a tangible example with which the reader can identify. For example, you might use the death of your pet hamster as a starting point for a discussion of religious philosophy. Remember, too, that admissions officers are pressed for time. They don't have all day to kick back and mull over your deep, brilliant insights.

Interestingly, when we asked classmates to submit essays to us, more than one-third were "thought essays," and almost all were tough to read. But when admissions officers sent us their favorite essays, only one-tenth were on philosophical topics. After all, if you were forced to read 300 essays a day, would you rather read Immanuel Kant or Mark Twain?

We don't want to scare you, though. The "thought essays" in this section are both interesting and effective. The first essay, *Do you think it's wrong*, succeeds by using a light writing style to discuss a heavy topic. As an admissions officer at Oberlin said, "Her essay is simply a reflection of the musings that go on in her head, which are quite impressive in their own right." He also noted that the essay was reinforced by the author's extensive involvement in programs for the poor in her community.

Melissa Holmberg's essay on black and white, and Phillippa Hollaway's essay on science and art discuss the realization that the world is not made up of opposites, but of shades of gray. Phillippa's determination to mix the traditionally separated studies of science and art shows a diversity most colleges applaud.

Jamie Mayer's inchworm essay—one of our favorites—is effective because it indicates, as his admissions officer said, "the ability to leave one's own perspective behind to see the world from the perspective of another age, culture, sex, or background. It shows unusual insight and perception, and the writing is simply superb."

The Development of an Idea by Eric Kaplan is probably not a viable alternative for most students. We read it with a dictionary close at hand. But once you understand his premise, you realize that his essay is an impressive piece of writing, exposing a brilliant mind. Nevertheless, if you are going to try an essay like this, watch out for syntactical clutter and pretentious allusions.

(Name Withheld)

"Do you think it's wrong to kill somebody if they're about to kill you but not on purpose?" — "How could I know that somebody's about to kill me if it's an accident?" — "Well, I don't know, but that's not the point." — "But you've got to give me an example." — "Okay, look—you're tied to the platform of a circular saw—" — "What? Who tied me there?" — "It doesn't matter. The operator of this saw doesn't know you're there—he's got his back to you—and he's about to set the saw going, but you have a gun in your hand and can shoot him if you like." — "Why would whoever tied me up leave me a gun?" — "I don't know." — "Why didn't I shoot *him*?" — "I don't *know*. Maybe you forgot how. But now you've remembered. 'Aha, that's it, I just pull the trigger,' you realize, and here is this perfectly innocent circular saw operator about to make cold cuts out of you. Would you kill him?" — "No—I'd yell and get his attention." — "No good, he's deaf." — "Well, then, I'd shoot him in the leg or something and then he'd notice me." — "You are *so* uncooperative!. . . Okay, look. You have no gun. Your finger is on a button that will open a trapdoor on which this man is standing and drop him into a pool full of hungry piranhas..."

I remember that discussion quite well even though it happened over a year ago. It was one of the more elaborately absurd results of my family's trying to grapple with a matter of ethics, but it had a serious question at its core. We batted it back and forth for what seems like hours, but I still don't know the answer. I wish I did.

People keep telling us students that the most important thing is to ask the right questions rather than to know the right answers. But I've got a lot of questions by now, and I would like a few decent answers too. I'd like to know if it's wrong for me to kill somebody who's about to kill me by accident. I'd like to know if it's wrong for me to kill somebody who's about to kill me on purpose. I'd like to know if it's wrong for me to *hurt* that person.

I guess Gandhi would say it was. Maybe Christ would too. "I say to you not to resist the evildoer; on the contrary, if someone strike thee on the right cheek, turn to him the other also." But are Gandhi and Christ right? And if they are, does that mean it would be wrong for me to kick a would-be rapist in the groin? Was it wrong for Nicaraguans to take up arms against Somoza? Was it wrong for England to defend itself in the Battle of Britain? I've taken a self-defense course; I took it so that I'd be able to fight back; and if I'm attacked I *will* fight back. But that's just because there comes a point when I'd rather risk doing wrong than suffer—it's not because I know it would be right.

There are other things I'd like to know too. Some of them more immediately relevant than others. I could reel off a whole list of dicey issues, none of them especially original (sex, censorship, lending I.D. cards, buying fruit from Guatemala . . .), but what is preoccupying me at the moment, what I'd like to know right now, is—would it be right for my family to pay several thousand dollars more than a Canadian university would cost even with financial aid, probably, for me to go to Oberlin? How many Ethiopians could you feed with the difference? How many years of college could you put a budding Pakistani agriculturalist through? Of course, it's possible that I'd be of more use to the world after a major in Third World Studies than after a Comparative Development program at a small Canadian university—when I discussed this whole problem with my interviewer, he mentioned some fascinating overseas work or study possibilities, quite apart from the college's terrific academics—but it's in no way certain. I might well be happier—more challenged—more stimulated—but I don't know if it's fair to count that. Is it? Do I deserve it? Or is it just a luxury?

Of course you can't answer that. It's something I'll have to tackle on my own. And since I'm sure you have enough to read as it is, I shall cease my musings on paper and leave them to go on in my head. At least I'll have more time to weigh up the pros and cons than I would if I were tied to a circular saw.

Melissa Holmberg

"The sign of maturity is no longer seeing things as strictly black or white." Mrs. Dempsey's casual remark was more powerful than her most emphasized assertions. Startled by the statement, I expected my class to be also, but my friends remained indifferently silent. They must not have heard her, or were only concentrating on the mechanics of the college essay, but I was confident that she would say it again and this time generate a response. "Avoid trite language and include explicit detail," she cautioned, returning to her lecture on the college essay technique. I realized that the remark meant something only to me, the group was not interested in discussing it.

How come I had never thought about the meaning of "maturity" if it was so important to the way I saw myself? I knew that because I was mature I no longer resorted to fits of screaming or crying to have my way, I did not giggle when reproduction was discussed in science, and I felt comfortable if included in adult conversations, but these were simply some of the side effects of a much bigger change. Now I knew what that change was. I no longer viewed things as either black or white. I was able to accept ambiguity, to see shades of gray.

For the first time I recognized an aspect of my emotional growth. As a child my entire world had been divided into two categories, good and bad. Parents, grandparents, and friends were good. Doctors, dentists, and babysitters were bad. I liked Her because she had gone to Paris. I loathed Her because she kissed boys. There were no inbetweens. But now my outlook is not so simple and narrow. Maybe it was the impact of my grandfather's death, or my parent's high expectations, or just the knowledge and experience which is gained with time, that made these classifications unworkable. Whatever the reason, it no longer seems legitimate to separate my world in two with seals of approval and brands of rejection.

Now I try to look at people as people, rather than items to

be indexed and filed. My purest whites and darkest blacks have been reopened for consideration. Somehow my father is not the same almighty man he was when I was a child. His opinions are not worthy of my unconditional acceptance, yet they are deserving of recognition and consideration. Someone is not bad just because she drinks, or smokes, or lies, even though these may be faults. There are fewer right and wrong, good and bad, and more and more "maybe that is right for him, but it is wrong for me," "maybe that is good for me, but is bad for her." My mind is freer, my eyes are more questioning, and my world is more vulnerable.

Phillippa Holloway

In our society there is antagonism between people who study science and those who study art and the humanities. Each side considers the other alien and views their differences as irreconcilable. The question of why the division exists is important to me because I am trapped between these two worlds. I am a musician and enjoy art and literature. However, I find science, especially chemistry fascinating, I have spent a great deal of time examining the issues that have kept these worlds separate.

Ayn Rand approaches this issue in her book *Atlas Shrugged*. In this book, there are significant differences in attitude that separate the protagonists from the antagonists. The protagonists are able to appreciate the beauty in two different worlds: the world of science and the world of art and love. The antagonists do not participate in both worlds and feel animosity towards the one they do not understand. When Hank Rearden give his wife a bracelet that is the first article ever made of Rearden metal, she views it as ugly and worthless. Mrs. Rearden exchanges the Rearden metal bracelet for Dagney's diamond bracelet. Mrs. Rearden can appreciate the beauty of diamond. Dagney admires the Rearden metal bracelet because she can see the unique aspects of this creation.

The conflict between science and art is examined directly by C.P. Snow in his book *The Two Cultures*. Snow tries to find the reason for this conflict. He believes that the conflict is caused by a lack of education. Students are encouraged to specialize at an early age and therefore do not receive a broad education in both science and art.

I disagree with Snow. The fact that students are encouraged to specialize at an early age is a symptom of the problem rather that the problem itself. The difference between the two sides is how one perceives the inherent beauty in each. Robert M. Pirsig calls this beauty "Quality" in his book *Zen and the*

Art of Motorcycle Maintenance. Sometimes it is easier for a person to see "Quality" in art rather than in science or vice versa. Once a person can see "Quality" in both sides, the two sides are linked.

Pritjof Capra deals with this subject by linking eastern mysticism with physics in his book *The Tao of Physics.* He finds that many of the concepts of subatomic physics are parallel and, in some cases, identical to the basic principles of Hinduism, Buddhism and Taoism. An increasing acceptance of these ideas will lead to a changed view of reality which Capra examines in his second book *The Turning Point.*

Thus far in my life I have been able to span both the world of the arts and the world of science. I play the viola in three orchestras and I read extensively in a wide variety of subjects including philosophy, politics, classics, and fiction. I have a great interest in science in general and chemistry in particular. I have participated in a number of special science projects and activities and have always enjoyed the challenge of the seemingly endless frontier of science. Additionally, I participate in debate, which requires knowledge and skills in a wide range of areas. In each of these activities I have been able to contribute more extensively because of the many facets of my knowledge.

I will continue to think about the integration of arts and science because it is so important in my life. I am faced with this dilemma. What will I be "when I grow up"? Will I be a chemist? Will I be a musician? Will I have to choose?

Jamie Mayer

I showed myself an inchworm this morning and now I feel guilty. Walking up the road beneath the leafy ceiling, I stopped myself short, face-to-face with a solitary green strand. The strand squirmed slowly, waiting for me to look closer. It was an inchworm, but it was not inching. It was spiraling on a central axis, like a single, floating strip of DNA. I never would have seen this swiveling little guy had his plump, new body and its delicate thread which was attached to an overhead branch not been hanging directly in my path.

Our eyes work on a now-you-see-it, now-you-don't system. One either focuses on the very near, or, as too many people do, on the distant horizon, blindly pointed off in one direction or another. Because of our human-proportioned lifestyle, things on an inchworm's measuring scale lose their impact. It is a "man-sized" world—bigger and better, new and improved. An inch just doesn't get you very far in our age of jet planes, space travel, and olympic long jump records of over 29 feet. Man has developed a knack for using himself as a ruler against which all else is measured. How egotistical we are.

So this morning, after nodding goodbye to my small green acquaintance, who was still swirling about like a circus performer with a rope between his teeth, I continued up the road, determined to look outside the proportions of the world I had grown up with. It was difficult. My eyes fought for their right to look through, rather than on the air; to a careful observer it might have looked as if I had a severe focusing disorder.

I am guilty. Guilty of belonging to this self-centered group that imposes its measurements and physical limitations on the rest of the natural world. It's true that the plants and animals which we can and cannot see don't realize the structure we have dropped them into. I am glad of this. Even the dolphin, said to be one of the most "intelligent" creatures after man, can swim the ocean, oblivious to the cities, borders and rules men have set up for themselves. I envy the dolphin, slippery flippers paddling, silly without-a-care jaws grinning. Intelligence without useless complication.

There is a Dr. Seuss story about a goofy elephant named Horton who discovered a tiny universe existing on a particle of drifting dust. Only one of the dust creatures believes there is anything beyond the tiny sphere, but in order to save the "planet" from destruction, its inhabitants must be convinced of life beyond their own world. Similarly, our only hope is to learn to acknowledge the worlds which exist around us. The worm was not aware of me or the human-oriented world I live in, but because I am able to, I feel an important responsibility to respect and protect these parallel universes.

Eric Kaplan

The Development of an Idea

In this essay I'm going to trace as best I can the development of an idea I first thought of three years ago and its appearance in different guises since then. It isn't intended to present this idea formally but rather to use it as an example of how I think.

The idea is of a thinking agent who can modify his deepest beliefs, mental habits and tendencies merely by deciding to. He can therefore use his decision making faculty to alter itself and any future decisions it will make—including about what alterations it will make in itself. A similar situation fascinated me when I was twelve—that of a dialectic in which the two members would in turn not only advance a proposition but a theory explaining away why anyone would not believe it. The later idea is similar to this except the mutually undercutting participants are part of one system. I visualized it at first in terms of cybernetics—positive and negative feedback loops, self regulating systems and such. I think though, I went to the cybernetics because I had this idea partially formulated already and not the other way around.

Because the idea wasn't an assertion that this is the way people are or even an hypothesis—maybe this is the way people are—but just an idea that intrigued me. I thought about it a lot but discussed it hardly at all. When I was fifteen the philosopher Lillian Molnar was explaining Brentano's ideas about intentionality and I mentioned this to her as perhaps being the kind of concept that theory dealt in. It seemed to me at the time that there were philosophers who spoke only what they were certain of at the risk of loss of richness and those who talked about everything at the risk of saying meaningless or wooly things. I felt Ms. Molnar was more of the second type while most other people I knew were closer to the first.

When I was seventeen I became less concerned with the logic of this idea than with the ethical implications. Because it seemed to me that when growing up we *do* make conscious choices to be one kind of person or another who will in turn make choices. So I wrote a play about it. In it the main character's consciousness of his ability to choose his future paralyzes his ability to make moral choices. Ultimately, the members of the family establish the family as an entity that transcends them all and for which they do not take responsibility. It can modify itself but is less likely to do so because as an institution it is less malleable than an individual and not self conscious.

I have never accepted the idea of a personal unconscious on epistemological grounds. Last summer when attending a seminar on Culture and Creativity I wrote a paper on how it is possible that self-conscious role players (as described by Harre and Secord and Goffman) can not be cynical. As an answer I outlined my idea of successive conscious decisions to be unconscious of something. I feel this explains the mind as well as a reified Unconscious without having the same problems. This was the first time after I explained it to Ms. Molnar that I ever communicated my idea.

The last allusion I made to this idea was in a comic public speech I made at this same seminar. In it I described a machine that allowed a person to change his body just by deciding to and how a man turned himself into a human gyroscope and because he could not operate the machine in that form was stuck that way.

By now I feel that what started off as just an interesting idea is now a standard part of my intellectual equipment. I use it to understand the mind and to draw analogies to other areas and am constantly finding ideas similar to it in the most varied sources; for instance recently I've been reading Buddhist psychology which says the mind has no identity over time. While once I kept it to myself it is now something I am willing to share with others. I find myself empathizing with Nietzsche's comment to his own thoughts at the end of Beyond Good and Evil "nobody will guess how you looked in your morning, you sudden sparks and wonders of my solitude." This essay is a try at letting others guess.

The Activities Essay

More than any other topic, college applicants write about their activities. This makes sense, particularly if an activity takes up a lot of your time, but be careful not to just repeat what you've already said in the other parts of your application. The key is to *personalize* and *analyze*. Why do you like to wind surf? What does basketball do for you? As president of the Chess Club, what have you learned and what have you observed—and what does that mean?

Joe Clifford explains what sports really have taught him, not what sports are supposed to teach him. Joe challenges common cliches, and such an essay always shows that you've been thinking.

The poem on poetry is unique for its self-referential quality, and the final stanza especially shows skill. Sending a sample of your work in place of the standard essay—a series of photographs, a performance on videotape, a painting—is risky. But if the sample demonstrates genuine effort and talent and if it answers the essay question better than words, it can be very effective. Of course, if your activity is rockclimbing, it may be hard to fit a sample in the envelope.

The "activities essay" can embrace both the mundane and the bizarre. In the next essays, three students create memorable pieces out of seemingly boring topics—cooking, day care, and babysitting. But each essay reveals its author's personality as well as any piece could. If you feel your life is just too conventional to write about, pay close attention to these essays. Imagine turning a basic recipe for cranberry bread into an effective presentation of your life! With a little creativity and a lot of hard thought, no topic is too dull for a great essay.

To answer the question "What famous person would you like to meet for a day?" one applicant dared to pick John Ellman, an 18th-century shepherd and breeder, and he proceeded to defend his choice intelligently.

Amidst repeated requests to meet Jesus Christ, Abraham Lincoln, and William Shakespeare, this essay must have really stood out.

David Meyer's defense of stamp-collecting pumps life into a paradigm of trivial pursuits. First, he demonstrated perseverance in creating an incredible collection, and then he showed he had thought a lot about *why* he had persevered.

Finally, John William's stirring essay on swimming for the gold indicates hard work and exciting goals. Not only is the piece a tautly written account of an exciting event, but it also reveals a vibrant, committed personality.

Joe Clifford

I am not sure how meaningful this is, but, if I were given the option of being either a well-reknowned intellectual giant or a Cy Young Award-winning baseball player, I would instinctively choose the latter. Sports, especially baseball and basketball, have played a very important role in what college application forms would call "my development as a human being."

When my father was teaching me how to play baseball, he would have me get into a batting stance with my whiffle bat. Then he would purposely throw the whiffle ball directly at the bat so that I could not help but get a hit. Of course, Dad would act exasperated, putting on his "How is a five-year old kid hitting like Babe Ruth against me?" routine. The point is, not suspecting that anything was amiss, I was in my glory. Here I was, five years old, and I was laying waste to anything my six foot, 200 pound father had to offer. Even my young mind appreciated the distinct Oedipal irony. This was heaven.

As I grew older (and began to understand why I was not hitting as perfectly as I had that first day) I continued to crave the black-and-white conflicts of sports. To this day, I still play the same David and Goliath mind-games that I first played with Dad hurling the old whiffle ball at me. For example, if I'm dribbling the ball towards the hoop in a basketball game, I'm saying to myself, "Here's little Joey Clifford taking it in to that intimidating behemoth from Midtown. Oh Goodness! Did you see that? Clifford just destroyed the goon with that sensational move! What a performer!" These mind-games are even more common when I'm pitching in a baseball game. For instance, I'll picture tomorrow's newspaper write-up in my head as I pitch. "Little Joey Clifford was just sensational out there," gushed Coach Jones, "after the fourth time he struck out last year's MVP I just said, 'Holy Smokes, what a performer!'"

I have written about these David and Goliath mind-games I play because they in particular emphasize why sports have been so important in my life. The way I approach sports has been a major influence on the way I approach life.

First of all, I am not the type to say that being a point guard has taught me discipline or that being a pitcher has taught me self-control and balance. I consider sports to be too pure and clean for that kind of specific and corny dissection. But, more generally, I cannot deny that sports have been the crucial factor in how I view life and how I accept challenges of life.

Sports have been called a "microcosm of life." I totally disagree. Baseball games are played in black-and-white in my mind. Life is one big gray area. Sports are simple and direct. Life is not. By way of contrast, sports have shown me that I cannot view life as a "me against the world" proposition as I would on the pitching mound. It is too selfish and egotistical a view for the "real world."

However, there is one area in my life where the David vs. Goliath motif that I learned through sports can be positively applied—how I accept challenges. As the weeks tick by in my senior year, the new challenges multiply at an alarming rate. And I like to accept each of these challenges as though I were the underdog, the "David" so to speak. (I picture a movie poster. "They said it could not be done. But he surprised every one of them.") However, it is in the solving of challenges that these self-serving mind-games have to be thrown out. Dad is not throwing the ball at my whiffle bat anymore. I can accept a challenge as if it were a baseball game. But I cannot solve it by striking someone out. This is what sports have taught me.

(Name Withheld)

On Poetry

Close your eyes to baited line,
And to the interweaving rhyme,
Seek not to capture clouds of time,
In metrics of a tortured prose.

For dabbling in this dainty game,
Without belief or teeming brain,
Is but to meddle — not to gain
Against the silence which now grows.

It is not on the written lines,
But in the caverns of the mind,
Where such thoughts are intertwined;
There the writhing serpent rose.

As all who've played the game before,
Who've tamed the rushing tidal roar,
And taught the condor how to soar,
— As any master poet knows:

Don't start with canvas start with dreams,
It is from these the artist gleans
The varied sequence of his scenes,
— Where grows the lawn the poet mows?

Written as a preface to a directed study I did in poetry. I read
the poetry of about ten modern British poets, from Hardy to
Thomas and by experimenting with their forms, meters, and
styles attempted to gain a greater control over language, and
isolate my own poetic voice.

Barbara Bluestone

Cranberry Bread

4 c. flour	1 small can frozen orange juice
2 c. sugar	4 T melted butter
3 t. baking powder	2 eggs
1 t. salt	1 c. chopped nuts
1 t. soda	1 pkg. cranberries

I'm not sure that cooking best reflects my personality; I am certainly not the domestic type, but I do enjoy cooking and baking if only because it gives me a chance to meditate and do something constructive at the same time. I think that my personality is what I think of when I have free time to ramble. Not only is the following an overview of my personality but also a delicious recipe.

First the flour and sugar need sifted together into a large bowl. Flour reminds me of the powder snow that falls in the West. I was born and raised in Pennsylvania where our snow falls more like sugar, granular and icy, and makes us hardy skiers unlike those spoiled by Western snow. Cold weather also is conducive to reading, which I love to do. I received my first Bobbsey twin book on my sixth birthday and have read my way through birthdays ever since. I just read *A Room With a View* by E. M. Forster and adored it. The baking powder, salt, and soda go in next. I have ceased to measure these any more. My mother taught me that to estimate is easier and sometimes the recipe will turn out better for an innocent mistake and a little adventuring. Always adding more chocolate is one of her ideas of an innocent mistake.

The orange juice needs to be thawed, opened, and added. Orange juice makes me think of poetry. The color is vibrant and the taste is sour, sweet, and tangy all at the same time, just like poetry. I write it and read it in search of new ideas and emotions—writers like John Keats, Emily Dickinson, T.S. Eliot, and Wallace Stevens never let me down. My own poetry allows me a freedom that is not there in prose, ideas that conflict or are confused can just add to the richness of the poetry. The butter needs to be melted, probably a microwave would be easiest. Technology, money and the free market system has done some wonderful things, not just for the art of cooking obviously. When I was younger, I liked to sit on my daddy's lap while he read the newspaper and he would explain to me what the stock market was, the meaning of options, the Dow Jones, etc. I still enjoy watching the stock market and I hope to do a mentorship with a stock analyst this year. All this would account for my goals of majoring in economics and then to work for my M.B.A.

The two eggs should be added to the bowl next. Then the nuts need to be chopped and put in the bowl. My little brother dislikes nuts immensely. He feels that I have betrayed him because I like nuts now, when before we were united against mom for putting nuts in chocolate chip cookies. Jonathan (my brother) calls the school I go to the 'Geek School'. He is wrong. My school is a mix of people that might not know where they are going but they know that they are going somewhere. If I didn't attend the North Carolina School of Science and Mathematics, I know that I would be jealous of those who did. The atmosphere of purpose that exists here is one I hope to also find in college.

The last ingredient is cranberries which need to be chopped in half before being added. Cranberries are autumn which is my favorite season. Fall is cool and shrewd and alive with those who can survive winter.

Grease and flour pans before putting mixture in. Bake at 350° for 50 minutes. Eat well.

Chris Gondek

Observing Me on a Thursday

It isn't very hard to get a valid impression of my personality by just watching me on an average day. However, the
best day to watch me is Thursday, as it provides me with am-
ple situations to present my many sides.

First, on Thursday, my alarm goes off at 5:45 A.M. This is a
daily ritual. One I so despise that I've mastered the technique
of terminating the clock while remaining asleep. Ten minutes
later, I decide to crawl out of bed, to go upstairs, and to bow
to society's whims by brushing, bathing, dressing, and eating.
Another twenty minutes go by before I act on this decision
though, and I rush out in a dagwoodian scene and arrive at
work at 7:00 A.M.

I am employed at a day care center, and being the second
teacher there in the morning, I deal with 25 first through
fourth graders who regard me as a surrogate victim to the
things they're going to do to their teachers at school. They
usually leave before I make any radical ethical re-alignments,
and I spend the rest of the morning with a group of lively
three year olds called by the code name, "Chipmunks". I've
learned a lot from them: I can name *every* He-Man figure sold
in North America. I know how to separate Crayola crayon
from a child's teeth. I can set up a snack with freshly made
punch for twenty in about five minutes. I can even analyze a
child's malady by simply looking at them. (Before snack,
stomach ache; before calendar time, fever; before clean-up, full
bladder; and before coloring, headache), something very few
applicants could dare say.

Fortunately, the other teacher with the three year olds is as
crafty, if not more so, as I am, so we usually survive the mornings. I end my first shift at 12:30 by putting a little elf named
Jack Hardcastle to sleep. Jack and I have one of those special

teacher-student, love-hate relationships. I dote on this little Artful Dodger, while he vomits, slaps, hugs, spits, giggles, jumps, and swears at me. He's a boy after my own heart, even though I've occasionally threatened to mail him to an economically deprived country.

My second shift starts at 3:00, when the first through fourth graders return from school like Marines on leave. Following afternoon snack, we usually delve into the world of art by doing cut and paste (something I hate) or by watching a movie. Originally, Debbie, the other teacher, and I tried to win them over to literature, but this was futile. However, should their behavior stray, I threaten to read Dryden's translation of Plutarch aloud. So far, this has proven effective. These children have taught me how to listen and handle criticism, since second graders don't censor their disapproval. I can do work in the loudest of conditions and I can say without reservation, that this has been the greatest experience of my life. I know the joy and pain of a child, and I'll never deprive my children or myself this knowledge.

After work, I drive home, watch the news, eat dinner and during the fall semester, go to class. My history class was my one night a week when I could spend time with intelligent people with a common interest. During breaks, our informal discussions ranged from 3rd Century Grecian pottery to bourbon as a decongestant. I got to know Professor Kounas well enough to know that should I be accepted, I'd like to seek out such a relationship again.

After class, I would come home and sleep, only to think of counsels and Kool-Aid and Lemon Bourbons and . . . 5:45 A.M. once again.

Jillian B. Myrom

It seemed I was there every hour of every day of every week when I was in the thick of it. But not for much longer! Today, August 8, 1985, was the last day I was babysitting for the Bowdens. And thank goodness! No more getting up at 7 a.m. on a summer morning, no more peanut butter and jelly every day at noon. I was through with all that. Moving on and moving up to better things. I had a job at Roy Rogers all lined up for me to start the following Monday. Finally, a real job.

I sat down hard in the metal chair in the Bowden's kitchen and glanced up at the clock. Four thirty-seven, only 53 minutes until Mom and Dad would pull up, hand me a check, and send me home for the last time. Grasping a blue crayon, I leaned over to draw a flower for Anya on her large white paper. Anya was six years old, and handicapped with spina bifida. This caused her spine to curve, which affected her internal organs so much that she was incapable of going to the bathroom. She needed to be catheterized about four times a day in order to relieve her bladder and reduce the possibility of infection or virus. She looked to be closer to the age of three if judged by her size. Her eyes were almond shaped and her features chubby, giving a mongoloid appearance. But I always thought she was beautiful.

Aaron, her older brother by two years, came running into the kitchen, closely followed by his little brother B.J., who was Anya's age.

"Jill? Where are my drawings of Voltron? I want to finish them before Daddy comes home. He promised to photocopy them if I do them in time!" Aaron searched frantically through the shelves next to the sink.

"I don't think they'll be in here, Aaron. Let's check in the den." Aaron and his sidekick scrambled into the next room while I turned back to Anya.

"And as for you!" I beamed down at her eager little smile. I pulled her to my hip, leg braces dangling, and we waltzed into the den when B.J. shouted, "I found 'em, Aaron! I found 'em! Daddy'll be so proud 'cause we didn't lose them!" Relief flooded the youthful face of Aaron, replacing his worried expression of a moment before.

"What are all the pictures for?" I asked.

"We're gonna send them to Channel 29 for their Voltron drawing contest."

"Yeah! And if we win, our pictures'll be on T.V.!" B.J. added, handing them to me.

"Well, if it were up to me, I sure would put them on T.V.! These are great, you guys!" And they were. I never knew a six and eight year old could be so artistic.

"Let's play a game, Jill!" I wanna play 'Life'!" Anya sounded so excited that I figured I could play her favorite game just one more time.

"Do you guys want to play?" I asked, carefully setting Anya down against the sofa, mindful of her feeble legs. I saw the VCR clock silently turn to 4:45 out of the corner of my eye.

"Oops! You know what? It's quarter of five, and you know what that means!" I said, pulling Anya up to me again. "Time to cath you!"

I carried her up to her room and laid her down so that I could catheterize her. Anya was always so good about it, as she was about all of her health problems, such as the operations she'd had and the therapy that she required once a week.

Clutching her Cabbage Patch doll, she said, "You cath me and I'll cath Gilbert, O.K.?," turning her deep blue eyes to me for approval.

"Sounds like a good idea to me," I replied, musing that perhaps Anya wasn't such a burden after all.

We returned to the den to find the game already set up.

"We're all gonna play, O.K. Jill?"

"That's great—the more, the better!" I resat Anya by the sofa and helped B.J. count out the money.

"Jill? Can we go to the park tomorrow and eat lunch there like we did the last time? That was fun."

"You know what, you guys? I can't take you anywhere anymore because today is my last day here with you. Your mom and dad are going to take some days off to be with you guys." They all sat quietly for a moment (which, upon looking back, was quite rare).

"You mean you're not coming back? Why? Don't you like us anymore?" Aaron's pout troubled me more than his words.

"Of course I like you! It's just that your mom and dad won't need me anymore this summer, that's all."

"Oh." B.J.'s eyes were downcast as he absently fumbled with the cards.

"Come on, you guys! Don't look so sad! I'm still your friend. You can come see me working at Roy's! Maybe I'll sneak you some extra fries if you don't misbehave. Would you like that?" I leaned over and tickled a giggle out of Aaron.

"And you!" I said to Anya. "We've got to get you a pair of those funky chicken sunglasses! What do you say to that?" I pushed her hair behind her ear and got a big smile in return.

Then out of the blue we heard a car door slam and two pairs of footsteps on the back steps.

"They're home! Mommy and Daddy are home!" The two boys ran out to greet them while I pulled Anya to my hip for perhaps the last time.

"Hi Jill! How've they been? Not giving you too much trouble, I hope," Mrs. Bowden smiled, placing her thin briefcase on the kitchen floor with a smart click of metal on tile.

"No, they've been great." I attempted a smile as I placed Anya down in her specially-made chair.

Her husband filled out a check while I stood looking at the three children who felt like my own. They waited in the kitchen while I retrieved my sneakers from the den. I tied my shoelaces tightly while they thanked me for the help I'd given them that summer. I told them that it had been my pleasure, and realized subconsciously that I was speaking the truth.

B.J. then looked up from under his Phillies' cap and said, "We'll miss you, Jill."

Unable to speak, I hugged each of them before I left their house for the very last time. Moving on to bigger and better things.

Or so I'm told.

(Name Withheld)

(Question: If you could spend an evening with any famous person, who would it be and why?)

With such a valuable, one-time experience at hand, I would wish to spend not only an entertaining, interesting evening, but one which would also prove valuable, meaningful, and thought provoking. Such an evening might be fulfilled by dinner and conversation with John Ellman. Born on October 17, 1753 at Hartfield, England, Ellman founded the Southdown sheep breed and devoted his life to its improvement. It is for this devotion and acccomplishment that most Southdown breeders (including myself) respect Ellman. Beside the distinguished honor of meeting such a man, I have several reasons for wishing to spend an evening with the "Father"of Southdowns. I suppose the most valuable thing I might learn from Mr. Ellman would be his philosophy. As with all great men, the key to life is philosophy. I have read of, seen, and admired the results of Mr. Ellman's work. I have a philosophy and I live by it as well as raise sheep by it. Ellman was a master at what he did and at life as well, apparently; I should like to learn his secrets. Hopefully, I would find that my philosophy nearly matched his. As with all professions, sheparding has its technical as well as philosophical requirements. Being a well established and practiced shepard, Mr. Ellman would surely prove a great source of information and "tricks of the trade." A shepard can only be as successful as his techniques and knowledge of his stock and species. Mr. Ellman's technique in improving the breed would be well worth learning. An evening of just listening and nodding in assent to preaching and teaching not only yields feeling of inferiority for the listener but also a rather unilateral conversation. I might contribute to the conversation by explaining the modern trends toward "quantity over quality" in the South-down breed and show him a picture of the modern Southdown. At this point, I could gain some direction and goal in the improvement of my flock by asking how he would like the breed to change. The remainder of the evening might be allotted an entertaining exchange of stories about sheep. The conversation would of course take place over a fat Southdown lamb dinner.

David A. Meyer

While many people consider philatelists slightly crazy for our attachments to those tiny bits of paper, I can say from experience that we are some of the most sane people in the world. We recognize a fun, educational hobby and partake with relish. For me, that hobby, more than any other I can imagine, widens one's imagination and greatly increases one's scope of knowledge. It has had a great effect on my own life, opening doors to countries that otherwise would have remained unknown to me, increasing my understanding of history, politics, and economics, and developing in myself a sense of world heritage. The hobby is one of the most all-encompassing and self-directed in the world, and its diversity can clearly be shown through my own collecting interests.

For years I have been fascinated by the languages, cultures, and history of Western Europe. When I started stamp collecting in the fifth grade, I began, like nearly all collectors, with a worldwide collection, but I soon began to narrow my range. For my fourteenth birthday, I received a large album for all German stamps. Since then I have developed collections of Austrian, French, Luxembourg, British, Channel Islands, U.N., Canadian, and U.S. stamps. The overall collection is fast approaching 21,000 items with my U.S. collection naturally the most complete. However, since I started collecting I have had the opportunity to visit post offices at the U.N. in New York as well as in Canada and most notably France. In my collection, the stamps I bought in their countries of origin have a special value, but so do those I have bought via mail from the post offices of Western European countries. For four years I have received mail from the post offices of Belgium, France, and Austria among others, some written in the native language of the country. I have enjoyed the practical use of my study of French and my attempts at German translation. The education I have received from my business transactions and my contacts with other countries in irreplaceable.

It is impossible to tell how much I have gained in my life through my collection. I can follow the struggles for independence of countries from Algeria to Zimbabwe on their stamps as well as the accompanying name changes. Costumes from Eastern Europe and Africa, landscapes of far-away countries, war heroes and heroes of peace, presidents, prime ministers, and patriarchs all peep from the pages of my albums. I have developed a good sense of geography and now recognize names and have an interest in countries in the news. For instance, when a cyclone hit the tiny country of Bangaladesh last May, killing 10,000, I could immediately picture the country because I remembered a map of it on a stamp. Through the inflationary issues of the 1920's, I can trace the fall of various currencies. German stamp values ranged from one or two marks in 1920 to one or two million marks only three years later in 1923. I even own a 20-billion mark stamp, today equal to six billion dollars but then worth only five dollars in U.S. currency. My collection has added to my appreciation of history and afforded many enjoyable moments. Several weeks ago I received an order containing several British stamps, among them a G.B. #3. This stamp, issued in 1841, was the third issue of stamps in the entire world. The thrill it gave me to hold it in my hand was inimitable. In sum, I believe that my favorite hobby has served to enrich and widen my view of life and in retrospect I am proud of what I have learned.

John M. Williams

It is the last hour of the last day. This is the showdown of the world. Every country is focused on this event and now it has arrived. My coach is quietly pacing up and down in front of me as we wait for my event to be called. I am oblivious to the world around me and I am mentally going over what I have to do in the next few moments to come.

I see myself start off with the quickness and agility found only in that of the fastest cats of the world. The hitting of the water sets me in motion. It is my only goal to finish first and to be the fastest. I see myself starting to the surface of the water and begin working as hard and as smoothly as I can. My arms and legs are ready for this and now it has come. Four long, hard years it has taken and now nobody is going to take this moment of glory away from me. I see myself going faster than I have ever gone before. Now there is nothing else but this moment, this feeling that has suddenly come upon me and told me that I am going to make it and prove to myself and to the world that I am the best.

The wall comes closer and closer. Then, with the grace of a ballerina, I flip and push off the wall. Now my body begins to build up even more speed. This is the last lap that I have to swim. I look ahead of me and nowhere else. I just keep look-ing down this tunnel into the distance. Like a light in the darkness, the finish appears. I start working even harder and every muscle in my body screams for oxygen. Harder and harder I work until I realize that the wall is almost in front of me. Then, with a last mighty lunge I reach for the wall. Thwap! I hit the wall and look around to see how well I fared. First place . . . I didn't see or hear anything around me. Just this feeling of euphoria.

Then slowly I come out of my trance and into the room with its cool comfortable walls and soft floors and realize that I was visualizing what was to come. I look at my coach and see him staring at me. He has stopped pacing the floor and is listening. I hear it too.

"Event number 100. Men's 100 meter freestyle. Swimmers please report to the blocks." As I rise to leave my coach looks at me amd says, "Go for it kid. It's all yours." As I open the door, the warm sunlight streams into the room and I look back at my coach and give him the thumbs up. Silently, without a word, I walk out to where the crowd is beginning to clap and yell as the names are announced over the loudspeaker. I hear my name mentioned and a feeling of pride washes over me as I enter the pool area.

Slowly I walk to where I am to start. I look back one last time and see my coach just sitting there quietly, watching and waiting. It is up to me now. The countless hours my coach has yelled and screamed at me have come down to this last moment in history. I begin stretching very slowly and concentrating on the next few moments to come. Firmly, I place my goggles on my head and look down to the other end of the pool that appears so far away. Then I lower them over my eyes.

Over the loud speaker I hear, "Timers and judges check your watches." I silently step up onto the blocks and the crowd has suddenly gone quiet. Then comes the final command, "Swimmers, take your marks." Slowly, I come down and cradle the blocks in my hands. My mind and body are one now and will be off with the sound of the gun.

"BANG." The sound recoils through my brain as my body lurches forward into the air and into the pool. I begin kicking as soon as I hit the water. My arms begin working in the quick, strong motions that have been grilled into my brain. I see the wall and realize that it is nearing faster than I had expected. I reach it and do my turn with a velocity so terrible that I create a humongous wake as I start down in the other direction. My body begins to pick up momentum even faster now, and I work it harder than I ever have in my life. My adrenalin bursts into my body and I go even faster. The wall is approaching and I don't even bother to slow down, just keep going right smack into the wall and finish.

Slowly, I raise my eyes and look around and see everyone has finished and I know inside my heart that it is going to be extremely close. As I look up I see my coach crying and smiling. I get out of the water and he says, "Congratulations kid, you did it!" I stare at him and then begin to cry as my name is called over the loudspeaker. Slowly I look around and everybody is yelling and cheering. Through the tears streaming down my face I see the American flag rising up and I salute it proudly. I had done what I had set out to do. All the training had paid off. There was nothing else but this.

I had won the gold medal in the 1988 Olympic Games. This was the zenith of my life. I go to accept my medal and stand proudly on top of the risers and I thought to myself of how proud my family would be now. Later that evening as I lay in bed reminiscing on what happened today I gently touch the medal that lay on my chest and peacefully fall asleep.

Before You Finalize and Mail It

1. Double-check for spelling, grammar, and punctuation mistakes.

2. Check for wordiness. Most essays could make their point more effectively if they were about half as long.

3. Make sure the essay looks neat.

4. Make sure you are satisfied with the essay. Does it reflect your personality and how you want to present yourself? Can you say, "This sounds like me"?

5. Photocopy the essay and the rest of the application, sign it, and mail it. Good luck!

Descriptive Essays

For sheer reading pleasure, these are our favorite essays. Rather than talking about themselves directly, these writers used telling descriptions of other people and places to reflect their own personalities. Don't forget that the essay should reveal something about *yourself*, so if your descriptive essay tells more about Kansas (or Grandma, or a cathedral you visited) than it does about you, it may be a waste of time.

Maeve O'Connor's beautiful essay tells a lot more about her own sensitivity than it does about her father. She manages to discuss an emotional subject without cliches, and she opens up to share something special with a reader who wants to be treated like a friend, and is.

Marie-Louise Buhler has created a character with a fullness usually found only in a short story. She has cared about someone enough to really think about him, a rare enough characteristic. In addition, her writing style is excellent. A writing expert at Yale explains that "the last sentence deserves reading and re-reading—for its stunning control of rhythm, and its wonderful ending on one lonely word (grammatically isolated, on the far side of a comma), 'alone.' "

The admissions officer who picked up the third essay probably thought: "Africa! Here comes some rich kid who's going to brag about his great vacation." But the piece works because it fools the reader. It says, in effect: "I'm not a spoiled child who thinks excitement only happens in a land far away." This essay encourages the reader to step back from his own 'ordinary' life, and discover how a new perspective changes the way you see things. Who would have thought that bubblegum could be so exciting?

With an effective metaphor, the writer of the fourth essay uses spice of life and curried chicken as appetizers to an essay on lunch. This writer understands the idea of synecdoche, the device of letting the part (two lunches) stand for the whole (two very different experiences). Her essay also demonstrates an admirable appreciation for diversity.

Jason Stuart's essay on Barbie employs an amusing irony. He manages to criticize society without sounding bitter or didactic. Students rarely write about "Big Issues" without losing themselves in tired rhetoric. If you want to talk about feminism or racism or poverty, try to relate the issue to something personal that you know well, and avoid the stale "Here's-my-plan-to-end-world-hunger" essay.

Peter Sweeney had the advantage of Grinnell College's unusually open-ended question which allows descriptions of both real and imaginary experiences, and he created an adventure that literally makes you shiver. Make sure your application allows this freedom before you start fantasizing!

The final essays could have been unimpressive, but both writers manage to tackle potentially trite subjects with skill. Catherine Sustana displays her fine writing ability in a unique essay of her family's annual trip west. Though admissions officers read hundreds of dull travelogues each year, Catherine's piece stood out because she describes herself as much as the sights. And Laura Stevenson, risking the "one-liner syndrome" (see page 15), makes a funny, insightful essay out of her daily family life.

Maeve O'Connor

Last Thursday was my father's birthday. I was standing on the sideline at my soccer game, shivering in the cold October drizzle, when suddenly I remembered. He would have been 53.

When I got home that day, Mom was in her room, sorting through some of my father's old sketch books. She had remembered too. I told her I thought we should spend the evening doing something Dad would have liked to do, and she smiled and said that was a wonderful idea. We selected a symphony by Beethoven from the stacks of records in the music room, and then the five of us gathered close around the small kitchen table for dinner. We ate by candlelight, laughing as we remembered.

No one had made a birthday cake, so when we had finished we went to Brigham's for ice cream. My father had loved to take us there on special occasions. I would have liked a dish of mocha almond, but I ordered chocolate chip with jimmies, just like I used to every time Dad took us to Brigham's when I was small.

It's cold out today, and I'm wearing my father's Irish sweater. He used to wear this sweater all the time on winter weekends. It has big holes in the shoulders that he never bothered to sew, but it's thick and warm, and our old house is drafty. In the past year or so, one of the holes has stretched so far that I'm afraid the entire sleeve will come off, but I don't want to mend it. I love the holes.

Marie Louise Buhler

He is the strangest person I have ever met, not simply eccentric, truly strange. He stumbled into my life (or rather I into his) the day Oma took me into that laundromat. With the wind at my back, I flew through the doors into a room of sticky, moist air that vibrated with the hum of a dozen different cycles. He was perched on the nearest dryer: checked shirt hanging open, light-blue polyester pants too high above the sockless feet encased in the inevitable sneakers. He guessed from my "outlandish" clothes that I was American (what other five year old in a small North German town would wear Raggedy-Ann skirts?) He asked on a hunch if I wasn't the little girl whose father was a lawyer in the Navy and whose mother was a friend of Uncle Gert, his own good friend. I was. Being a precocious child who told every embarrassing family secret to any stranger who cared to listen, I struck up a fine conversation with him. He complimented me on my German and then Oma towed me back out into the rain.

I never gave that incident another thought until Uncle Henry moved to the States to become an integral part of my Sunday afternoons and my family. I hear him laughing downstairs. I see his shoddy pants and frayed shirts, his silver hair as a Prussian soldier's (my mother says) and his round, red face with its little mustache. It's the face of an English squire. That's what he should be, a country lord with a fixed income and nothing to do but read and take long walks instead of eking out a living keeping books for Palmer Ford. I guess I really don't know much about him. Nobody does and that's the way he likes it. What I do know convinces me that if ever a man were born in the wrong century, it's Uncle Henry. He is a chivalrous knight. Once he was engaged and in love, but when he heard another richer man wanted to marry the girl he gave her up, *told* her to marry the guy and moved. Some people call that stupid, throwing away happiness with

both hands, and maybe it was, but it was *noble*. He says a
man's life is over at thirty-five unless he's married. Accordingly, he lives like monk, always refering to himself as "this old
man" and remarking that he can feel the "cool wind of the
grave" blowing towards him. His pleasures are mainly scholarly. He lives in his Shakespeare and his French studies. He also
lives in his coke and bourbon. Not, I guess to "wash the dust
of the road" from his throat, as he puts it, but to wash away
too vivid memories of war and of loss. And it works, and
remembering the good times and his beloved homeland, he
bursts into old German songs which he bellows at the top of
his lungs no matter where he is. When my sister and I were
little, he embarrassed us and we pleaded with Uncle Henry to
be "normal". He hasn't stopped laughing about that one
since. Our begging had no effect and I'm glad now; I love his
idiosyncracies. He is a Catholic who regularly speaks aloud
with God, whom he asks to forgive "this old man" for never
attending services. Evolution offends him, he won't even consider that we are related to animals. Uncle Henry believes that
he is, and he is, a race apart. On the subject of modern
medicine he is a skeptic, and though he should see someone
about his blood pressure, he has staunchly refused to do so for
the past twenty years. I love this man who sends me out of
the room when he is going to tell a dirty joke, who advises my
mother to give the two of us cold showers to keep us out of
trouble, who calls me his "pale beauty" and tells me to eat
more. Everybody likes him, but no one understands him. He
lets nobody in. And in the end all he has left are his books
and his bourbon and his memories, as he sits in a crummy
shack of an apartment with gaping holes in the roof, alone.

(Name Withheld)

For myself, living in Africa has given a commonplace quality to events that would be considered extraordinary in the United States. For example, at school pupils were occasionally assaulted by baboons, while in Nairobi bread and milk shortages were frequent. Similarly, on vacation from East Africa, there have been aspects of America's culture that seem alien and magnificent—

To me
The words
'Elizabethtown,
Lancaster County
Pennsylvania, U.S.A.'
mean two months every two years of reassuring luxury.

The immaculate green waves of corn form a secure wall
about the smooth macadam, as we drive in;
a sixty foot yellow 'M' to the left brings on a maniacal
craving
for a quarter pounder, and overweight women rock on their
porches
with a glass of iced tea, a bowl of pretzels.

The humid warmth feels relaxing the next morning;
in a T-shirt, a pair of slacks, and flip-flops, we walk up
the lane to the Hypermarket. Pure, white, neon-lighted
aisles;
things we dreamed of—watermelon and corn on the cob,
Grape Soda and pop tarts, bubblegum ice cream and Angel
Food Cake.

Staggering back beneath big brown packages, we look
at the trimmed hedges, spotless lawns; a polished
   Chevrolet
moves leisurely past, some kid floating behind it
on roller skates.

Later we sit wrapped in the reassuring and meaningless
colour of the television, absorbing 'The Price Is Right,'
our favourite game show, or Mork and Mindy. Of course,
   there's
a can of Mountain Dew balanced on our knees
while we chew a piece of Super Large, Grape Flavoured
                              Hubba Bubba Bubblegum.

(Name Withheld)

If variety is the spice of life, then my educational background must be equivalent to curried chicken. I have been fortunate enough to experience life at both a private girls school of 450 students (K-12) and a public high school of 1250 students (9-12). The differences between my years at the two can be summed up through one medium; a description of the lunchroom experience in each.

At private school, I dined everyday at precisely 12:30. All of the girls, or "little women" as the head mistress often called us, would waft into the diningroom and each would take her proper place, standing behind her assigned seat. After a few moments of our gazing demurely at the center of the room, our head mistress would appear there and ring a little bell to assure our attention. After a short but pious blessing, everyone would sit down and the meal would be served. Lunch was a family-style affair, so every table would receive three or four serving bowls of food. We dined using real silverware and napkins that were almost as starchy as the teachers who sat at the head of each table and served. The teachers were there to correct our manners and keep the conversation formal and polite. Many were the days when I tried to make interesting contributions to discussions of William Shakespeare's use of the preposition in "Hamlet." (I was assigned to an eccentric literature teacher's table.)

That is not to say that lunch at a private school can not be a fun event. The little women at my table and I would often compete to see who could shake the teacher's haughty calm. (It was quite fun, actually, when I was in the seventh grade.) The girl who sat across from me got the closest to winning when she "accidentally" flipped a pea into the air and it got stuck to the chandelier directly above us. She was proud of her perfect aim for days. When we finished dining (and playing), our head mistress would lecture us on our atrocious manners and then dismiss us with another tinkle of her bell. The dining process never varied from that course.

Lunch at a public school is very different. First, there is no dining room. Instead, we have a cafeteria. The distinction must be made. Also, nobody wafts into the room. The lunch-line into the cafeteria would be most aptly described as a stampede. Once one has his lunch, he may sit where he likes. He may even go outside and eat on the smokers' patio. When I first saw that patio during my first day at public school, I thought that the building was on fire. While eating, one may talk about whatever he likes, move about the lunchroom as he likes, or work on his homework. However, there are teachers who circulate around the room to make sure that no serious damage is done. If they catch a student misbehaving, the student receives a punishment known as lunchroom duty. That is when one must spend the last five minutes of the lunch period wiping crumbs off tables. It is my assumption that those being punished get extra-credit if they can manage to make the crumbs land in someone's lap. Even though I have never been assigned lunchroom duty, I have often been the prey of those expert crumb slingers who have. All in all, lunch at a public school is a wonderfully crazy event.

Both of the schools that I have described through their lunchrooms are very good academically. Their differing policies make each one special. One uses extreme discipline to stimulate students and the other uses freedom. Having attended both types of school has really helped me by the experience that I have gained. Attending the private school helped me to develop excellent study methods. Attending the public school may have helped me develop something even more important; a longing to do new things and meet new people. Attending Atherton High School gave me the incentive to travel freely around Europe with some young friends (which I did after my freshman year), take up scuba diving lessons, and learn how to snow ski. I know that attending Chapel Hill, if I am given the opportunity, could do the same thing.

Jason Stuart

If I were given the opportunity to spend an evening with any one person, living, deceased or fictional, whom would I choose and why?

She's about 5'9", has beautiful blond hair, and a beautiful figure. She's every boys grade school dream. She's the idol of thousands of young girls around the world. She's been a legend for the past 25 years. And she's the one girl I've always wanted to meet.

Her name is Barbie, and she's been on my mind ever since I saw her at my next door neighbors house ten years ago. Barbie's been mass produced by Mattel for 20 years. The advertizements have led me to believe that she is the perfect girl. She's beautiful, she lives in a house appropriately enough called a dream house, she has a dream job, and closets and closets full of dream athletic wear, swim wear, evening and casual wear. The woman is suppose to be what all little girls should grow up to be, according to Mattel at least. However for every lovely feature of Barbie that all little girls want to aspire to and all little boys want to aspire with there are others across America who feel differently. Many women feel she is cheap, ugly, fake, and that she stands for only material things. They believe that Barbie illustrates the idea that beauty is something you put on every morning.

However, if I was ever given the chance to meet anyone in the world I would pick Barbie. Ever since I was a young kid in the second grade and I saw Barbie on TV in one of her many swim suits I've had this urge to meet her. What normal second grade boy wouldn't? She's perfectly proportioned, she has long blond hair, killer blue eyes, long slender legs, and she drives a Corvette! What normal male, for that matter, wouldn't want to meet Barbie!

Yet there is more than just a physical attraction between us.

All through history women have been dealt with as mysterious. Fathers tell sons that they will never understand women, that they are too complicated, etc. And from personal experience I can tell you that this is for the most part true. Yet, here is Barbie, the woman who embodies all that is feminine. Barbie has been put at top of the grand pyramid of women, she is what all women and girls should want to be; ambitious, beautiful, rich . . . perfect. It is my contention that Barbie is the key that will unlatch the years of mystery surrounding women, to unleash all that has gone unbeknownst to the male population since the beginning of time. If I were given a night to speak with Barbie, I'm sure I would wake up the next morning understanding exactly what women throughout the world were all about. Yes, I'm sure there are thousands of women across the US that would argue that Barbie is nothing but a cheap plastic doll degrading to the whole female population and who was put into production only to excite the hormones of grade school boys all over the world. But what better reason to meet the woman. Here Barbie is at the crux of one of the greatest American debates of all time. Single handedly this woman we call Barbie has set mothers versus daughters all over the nation. This woman has set the female population on its ear. No one knows what to believe. Is Barbie (bleach) or was she born blond? Is she incredibly fake and stupid or is she an ambitious working woman? I say it doesn't matter either way. Barbie has received more attention and more debate by the human race than any president, millionare, or rock star. Anyone who has been talked about and fought over as much as Barbie, certainly will have something worthwhile and interesting to say.

Well, as you can probably tell I am one of those pro Barbie people. I do believe in her and what she stands for and this brings me to the last reason I want to meet her. I don't want to see Barbie make a mistake. She still hasn't married Ken. Now they've been going together for some time now but to my knowledge, they still haven't tied the knot. I wouldn't be able to stand seeing my Barbie get married to someone as fake as Ken. As far as I can tell, the guy doesn't have a job, he doesn't drive, and Barbie's the only one with a checkbook. I've never seen Ken pick up a tab for Barbie on TV. As far as I'm concerned, he's a gold digger. He doesn't even have real hair, he's got groved plastic, painted dirt brown for a head.

If I could possibly meet with this woman for one night, just one, and if I told her my feelings towards her relationship with thousands of women and girls throughout the world, and if I could tell her just how big a mistake it would be to marry a guy like Ken, I would feel I had made a great contribution to humanity, as well as to myself, by picking up some valuable information on the way.

Peter Sweeney

My pick bit into the ice with a sharp cracking sound. I tested my weight experimentally on the line before I slowly pulled myself onto the ledge, every fiber in my arm aching with the effort. I retched miserably, but nothing came up. I was tense and I was cold, two very dangerous traits when climbing in the Swiss Alps. I knew that I was exhausted, both mentally and physically, yet I could not go back. Wearily, I prepared myself for the next cliff.

Two hours later, I had climbed that many hundreds of feet and once again crawled onto a thin ledge. I was shaking uncontrollably, not so much from exhaustion, but from the piercing cold that cut through my jacket like lancets hurled by the wind.

The Wind! Of all my enemies—exhaustion, hunger, pain—he was the deadliest. He numbed my arms, my legs. He took hold of my brain, tricking me into thinking I was dreaming, goading me to let go of the rope, the pick. He swirled about me, unseen, yet felt. He forever taunted me, screaming at me to give up. He tore at my fingers, pulling, straining, ripping at my numbed members. He howled mightily, trumpeting his superior might.

But did he reckon with the human spirit? . . . that ineffable quality in all men, which supports them and urges them to put up a fight—a fight against the Wind, the emissary of death, against injustice, treachery. That one quality which sets men apart from all other elements of nature: the will to survive, to fight for their lives and their rights.

Mine was the right to live. Yes, the Wind knew about bravery and determination, and he knew of its power. He did not oppose it, but attacked the weaker side of man. The side which desired: desired food, sleep, warmth. Like the Serpent of old, the Wind tempted man, taking away that precious warmth and tricking him into the numbness of the Void.

I awoke with a start. I was conscious of the hard ground beneath me and then the wind and the cold. It had become noticeably darker, and I realized how dangerous my situation was. If I did not reach the lodge at the top of the mountain before nightfall, I would find myself in a perilous situation— the bitter cold, coupled with the totality of darkness would increase my chances tenfold of missing a crack and falling to my death. Slowly, I sat up.

My arms were stiff and night was rapidly approaching. I was in a hurry to reach the top, and in my haste, I was careless. Halfway up the next cliff, my pick slipped and fell. I hit the ledge I had just left 80 ft. below me with a jarring shock. I felt my head crack against the ice and darkness enveloped me.

When I slowly surfaced from that hazy gray world of unconsciousness, I discovered that I could not open my eyes. They felt leaden. I slowly brought a gloved hand to them and rubbed them feebly. They opened unwillingly.

A long time had passed since my fall, for by now the sky was black as pitch. I could see only this much for my eyes closed quickly, exhausted by their effort. I fought desperately against unconsciousness but it was useless. I fell once again into the abyss of nothingness.

I awoke shaking and sweaty. My back throbbed with a dull pain and my head felt as if it had been worked on by a blind barber. I could no longer feel my legs beneath me except for a pain in two places below my right knee, both of which burned with a fierce frozen fire. Very slowly, I worked myself into a sitting position, leaning back against the same cliff that had cruelly betrayed me.

I eased my pack from my back and hastily ripped it open. Most of its contents were wet from lying in the snow for so many hours, but I knew that I had a set of waterproof matches in it. Frantically I searched for them as a drowning man will search for land; but they were not there. My anxiety intensified, the fog in my brain darkened, and I spilled the contents of my back onto the ledge, fumbling through them. With dawning horror, I realized that I no longer had them. How I had lost them I would never know. I screamed aloud in utter frustration and despair. The Wind screamed back in triumph. Without any source of warmth, we both knew that I would not last long.

And oh Christ, it was cold.

Catherine Sustana

We always said we'd leave in the morning, but we could never wait. By four o'clock in the afternoon we were piled into the station wagon, Charlie McCoy playing on the stereo and the U-Haul humming behind us on the highway. We roared straight into the sunset, straight into our impatient adventure on I-40 West.

I couldn't sleep. This was tradition; I had to stay awake to see the Mississippi. The headlights, smooth and hypnotic, flashed by us in the opposite lane, growing thinner as the clock hands moved forward. The stereo had long since been turned off. My father was silent, and I watched my mother's head bob as she passed in and out of consciousness. I leaned forward and rested my chin against the front seat, staring into the black, foggy curves of the Smoky Mountains and waiting for the bridge.

When I woke up, the sun was pink and cool and flat. I looked out the windows and tried to imagine how far we had come. Oklahoma was flat and cool in the morning, like the sun. The tobacco farms had changed to ranches, and the sky had spread itself far into the corners of the horizon, but I couldn't escape the feeling that I could walk home, that there was no distance.

This how every trip to the West began—a blind, passionate drive into Oklahoma ranches, Kansas wheat, Colorado mountains. We planned for weeks in advance, but the vacations always seemed spontaneous. This is where I first learned to trout fish, where I first saw beaver dams, where I first saw unexploited ghost towns. This is where we piled six people into a CJ-7 and bumped dangerously up Engineer Pass into the wilds of the Rockies, just the elk, the marmots, and the Sustanas. It was disorganized but heartfelt adventure.

The last time I visited the West I asked a friend what he wanted me to bring him. "Nothing," he said. "Don't bring me anything. Just write it all down, and remember it, and tell me everything."

I remember the way the clouds in New Mexico looked like a window that had just been hit by a baseball. I remember the way the two boys in Magdalena, Arizona looked after they had wrecked their motorcycle. They were dusty and dazed, and I wondered why they were carrying so much beer on a Sunday morning. I remember the Chicano children in the IGA in Winslow. I remember the jewelry makers and the Indians and the trading posts and the fishermen and the ranchers and the blacksmiths and the gold mines.

This is what's important—to remember it, to write it down. I have stories, stories from every trip West, from every street festival, from everyone I have met, and from every day that the wind blows just right and the whole town smells like tobacco. Sometimes I can't remember crossing the bridge, but I get there, and I can write. Writing is my blind, passionate adventure, my communication that turns the curves in the dark and invariably crosses the bridge.

Laura Stevenson

"Megan," I said, "If you were to choose one word to describe me, what would it be?"

Her eyes lit up. "Ugly," she replied, "Fat and Ugly."

"Ha ha, you're a funny one. Seriously, Meg, I have to write an essay about myself, and I need a word. Just one."

She frowned and thought for a while. "Funny," she finally replied. I looked at her, wondering if she was serious.

"Yes, Laura, you are funny. I've never known anyone who could make even the most depressing things seem slightly humorous."

This was a slap in the face. I was thinking more along the lines of brilliant, wise, loyal, trustworthy, responsible or wonderful. So much for friendship. It seemed sad that my very best pal could say nothing about me except that I had a warped sense of humor. Yet, after thinking about it for awhile, I realized that although it may not be as useful as an I.Q. of 160 or a perfect 1600 on the SAT's, this sense of humor has come in handy several times in my life.

Who could help but develop a sense of humor in a house of nine children, eight of whom are girls? I have to be humorous just to be heard. Our dinner table is about a mile long, and I need a megaphone just to ask for the mashed potatoes. Imagine doing calculus problems while four stereos are each blaring a different song. Or think about going into a shoe store with seven sisters, each needing her own "perfect pair." That's humor.

Growing up where eight just wasn't enough had its advantages. By the time I was in first grade, I knew the meaning of the word "crowd." Making friends was much easier. It's also nice to have a personal cheering section at diving meets and soccer games, and to have at least five automatic buyers of anything sold by the National Honor Society. It is also very necessary to have a competitive nature in this sort of environment. Somebody has to get the last ice cream bar in the freezer. Don't get me wrong, life with eight other children isn't always a bowl full of cherries. It does have its pit falls. For example, try fighting a red head who is three feet taller than you are for the front seat in the car. Christmas shopping for just the family gets to be quite an expensive ordeal. And there isn't always a lot of personal attention. I have to wait in line just to talk to mom. All in all, however, I wouldn't trade in my family for anything. Life with a big family has taught me confidence, competitiveness, and a lot of humor which will help me with anything I choose to do.

About the Authors

Boykin Curry and Brian Kasbar are members of the Yale Class of 1988. They grew up together in Summit, New Jersey, and both plan to pursue entrepreneurial careers when they graduate.

More Great Books
from Mustang Publishing

The Student's Guide to the Best Summer Jobs in Alaska by Josh Groves. Thousands of young adults head for Alaska each summer, seeking jobs in the lucrative fishing industry. This book offers the most accurate and thorough information on the Alaska summer job scene available. Don't go to Alaska without it! *"Highly recommended"—The Tartan, Carnegie-Mellon Univ.* **$7.95**

Europe: Where the Fun Is by Rollin Riggs and Bruce Jacobsen. No hotels, no museums, no historic sights—just the best bars, nightclubs, restaurants, beaches, flea markets, etc. all over Europe. Just the fun stuff, in an entertaining and irreverent style. The perfect supplement to the major European guides. *Named one of the 25 best European travel guides by Changing Times Magazine.* **$7.95**

The Complete Book of Beer Drinking Games by Andy Griscom, Ben Rand, and Scott Johnston. Attention party animals! With 50 of the greatest beer games in the world, this book has quickly become the beer drinkers bible. Over 60,000 sold! *"A classic in American Literature"—The Torch, St. John's Univ.* **$5.95**

Beer Games II: The Exploitative Sequel by Griscom, Rand, Johnston, and Balay. The uproarious sequel to *The Complete Book of Beer Drinking Games* is even funnier than the original! 30 new beer games, more hilarious articles and cartoons, and the wild Beer Catalog, which must be seen to be believed. *"Absolutely fantastic!"—34th Street Newspaper, Univ. of Pennsylvania.* **$5.95**

Mustang books should be available at your local bookstore. If not, you may order directly from us. Send a check or money order for the price of the book—plus $1.00 for postage *per book*—to Mustang Publishing, P.O. Box 9327, New Haven, CT, 06533. Please allow three weeks for delivery.